MIND GAMES

Mind Games

a Jen Rice novel

SHANON L. MAYER

Shanon Mayer

First Printing, 2024

Cover design by JD&J Design

ISBN: 978-1-958076-15-6, 978-1-958076-16-3, 978-1-958076-17-0

Published by Shanon L. Mayer, Vancouver WA 98663

https://shanonlmayer.com

Books by Shanon L. Mayer

<u>Chronicles of the Chosen</u>
Sphere of Power
Veil of Deception
Reflections of Doubt
Palace of Stone

<u>Jen Rice</u>
Captives and Prisoners
Festival of Souls
Beautiful Monsters
Mind Games

<u>Inland Sea</u>
Star of Darkness
Eyes of Midnight
Grand Coven

<u>Shadow Tribunal</u>
Diamond Queen

This is for everyone who waited patiently (or not so patiently, in some cases) for me to revise and continue with Jen's story. Thank you, all of you, for believing in me and trusting that I wouldn't just leave you hanging!

Special thanks to everyone who helped me with the stickiest bits, parts I wasn't sure how to handle. Your guidance and support helped to make Jen's world the place it is today and makes me excited to continue living in it and sharing it with all of you!

Chapter 1

David Melrose, Charlie Winters, and Marc Anderson sat in David's office on the third floor of the New World Response building. David sat in his high-backed chair behind his desk, which was overflowing with paperwork that he hadn't been able to get caught up on yet. He had his feet up on the table, his heels resting on yet more paperwork that Charlie had brought for him that afternoon. His dark hair had started to grow out from the short, neat haircut that he had maintained for the last year and as he brushed his hair out of his eyes, he looked over his desk for his day planner. He really needed to schedule that haircut he had been putting off.

Charlie sat in one of the comfortable guest chairs that rested opposite David. He was dressed in his favorite charcoal grey suit but today he had brightened it up with a lively red tie. The only indication he gave of having not slept the previous night was the hint of stubble that was barely visible on his normally clean-shaven face.

Marc paced restlessly across the room. He was the only one of the three that wasn't dressed in a suit. Instead, he wore the black uniform of the New World Response team, of which he was the unit leader.

"You know they're going to get the court order sooner or later," Marc pointed out to the other two as he paced. "Todd's got them held at bay for the moment, but we all know that won't last long."

"Like I told you," Charlie turned his head to watch the pacing man, "if they were going to get a court order, they would have done it by now."

"I know," Marc said, "but now they want to bring in some sort of a specialist to see her? It's only a matter of time before they get their stooge to say she needs more than North Bank can provide. With their doctor in their corner, it won't matter what Todd says, they'll just take her anyway."

Charlie shook his head. "Greg's a good guy; he wouldn't do something like that." He looked down at the cup of coffee on the desk in front of him. He picked it up to take a drink, but its contents had long since gone cold and he put it back down again. "That's why I asked him to take this case."

Marc stopped pacing and looked at him incredulously. "You asked for this?" He stepped closer to the seated man, incensed. "How could you do that?"

"Because she needs it, which you know every bit as well as I do," David interrupted. "You need to calm down, Marc." When Marc scowled but stopped pacing, David continued. "As far as I'm concerned, the argument over who is treating Jen is irrelevant. Our main concern should be for her and that she is getting the treatment she needs so that she can get better. The doctors who had been treating her are still there and Dr. McAdam has agreed to keep them in the loop on what's happening with her, and they are keeping us updated as well."

"Updates are nice but why hasn't she woken up yet? It's almost been a week."

"Think about it," Charlie said. "That girl just went through hell, quite literally. It's not really much of a surprise if she needs a break to process it all." He looked over at Marc and continued. "It's actually pretty common after a heavy trauma like what she went through."

Marc shook his head. "All of the others that we brought back with her are awake. Hell, most of them have already been released from the hospital and taken to that group home they're staying in."

"Exactly," Charlie said. "But Jen still isn't awake, so having a psychic come in to treat her is the best option for her right now. Like David said, our focus is on getting her better. The rest can be dealt with if and when it happens." He picked up his cup and poured more hot coffee into it to warm it up again.

"I asked Greg to come in on this for two reasons. First of all, he's one of the most experienced people out there dealing with paranormal trauma right now, which is exactly what Jen has." He sat back in his chair and took a drink of his coffee. "Secondly, Greg is all about the patients first. The NPIB may be paying him but Jen is his patient, not the NPIB. He isn't going to recommend that they do anything unless it really *is* in her best interest."

The National Paranormal Investigative Board was the governmental agency responsible for monitoring all of the paranormal activity in the country. Charlie was a staff analyst for the NPIB and had originally arrived in town on a recruiting mission to hire Jen Rice. However, when he arrived, he discovered that Jen was missing and had in fact been kidnapped by demons. She had been held in the dark realm known as Derathim for almost a month while her teammates at New World Response and her brother Todd, a powerful mage in his own right, searched for a way to find her and bring her home.

When they had finally succeeded in breaking through to Derathim, they had rescued not only Jen but over a dozen other prisoners that had been held alongside her. Torture by the demons, in some cases ongoing for years, had left both physical and emotional scars on everyone that had been held there. All of the prisoners were undergoing treatment at North Bank Hospital, the largest medical facility in the county. A few of the captives had already been released to a local care center for long-term treatment, which was more of a group home than a medical center.

Because of her exposure to the high levels of dark energy that were everywhere in Derathim, the NPIB had been pushing to have Jen transferred to one of their own facilities so that they could treat her for exposure before she woke up. Her twin brother Todd had been at her side through the whole process and had so far thwarted every attempt the NPIB had made to that effect.

Behind the scenes, David had been doing his best to help both Todd and Jen. There had been stories his entire life of people being transferred to one of the NPIB's secret facilities and never seen again. He wasn't sure how much faith he held in that happening but he didn't want to gamble Jen's life on it. To that end, he had arranged for Todd to have power of attorney, effectively putting the mage in complete control of his sister's care.

Through Charlie, David had discovered how angry that move had made the NPIB agents but by then it was too late. The most they could do at that point was to obtain a court injunction that would allow them to take her away. So far, they hadn't had any success in getting one.

At Charlie's request, Todd had relented enough to allow Dr. Greg McAdam, a physician who had been brought in by the NPIB, to take over her medical treatment. David still wasn't sure why he had agreed but Todd wouldn't have allowed it if he had any doubts about Jen's welfare. As far as David was concerned, if Todd was okay with the new doctor, he could be too.

Not that Todd had put complete faith in the new specialist, David realized. Whenever the physician was in the room to treat Jen, Todd made sure that there was at least one other person he trusted there with them. Although the mage hadn't said as much, David had gotten the distinct impression that Todd wasn't ready to trust anybody that was connected with the NPIB. That distrust extended to Charlie, although not to the same extent. Charlie had been around longer and Todd had been able to talk with the staff analyst often enough that he seemed willing to accept him, at least for the moment. Additionally, Charlie had entered Derathim alongside the New World team to rescue Jen and the others. That fact seemed to hold a little weight among Jen's family.

Finally, Marc relented. "So what's so special about this doctor, anyway?" he asked. "He didn't seem like all that much when I was there earlier."

"Actually, there are a few reasons," Charlie answered. "First of all, he's a specialist in wounds and injuries that are inflicted by magical or psychic attacks but he's pretty good at standard injuries also. Above that, he's a psychic, so he can treat the smaller stuff that she might need without having to do more damage with operations." He took another drink of his coffee and set the cup down again. "Even though it looks like Jen's been healing pretty quickly on her own, we couldn't be sure that the healing was everywhere or just on the surface."

"What does that mean?"

"Well, if she's just healing on the surface, there might still be injuries deeper inside of her that we couldn't find. Those might be a factor in why she hasn't woken up yet. For a regular doctor, the only options they have would be X-rays and CT scans until they found something. Those procedures are still harmful to the patient and the more times a person is exposed to them, the more damage they do. Plus, there's no guarantee that they'd be able to find out what was going on inside of her even with all the tests.

"Greg's different because he can look at her, look inside of her, to see all those things without having to expose her to all of the bad stuff."

"And that's what he's been doing?" Marc relaxed a little as he absorbed what Charlie was saying.

"He started with a list of possible injuries that he has seen in cases like hers and he's been eliminating each of those. After that, he's going to look into her as a whole and see what was missed with all of her other examinations. By the time he's done, she'll be healthier than she was before the demon took her."

"But will she wake up?"

"When she's ready to. Like I said, it's not

unusual for someone's mind to turn off for a bit when they've been through something traumatic. It gives them a chance to sort through everything and not have to deal with all of the outside crap while they're accepting what happened." He took another drink of his coffee. "Frankly, I'd be more worried if she hadn't shut down. That would mean that she isn't really dealing with what happened yet and she's more likely to have an emotional breakdown over it later, when it finally sinks in what happened."

"So you're saying this is actually good for her." When Charlie nodded, Marc thought for another moment. "Has your doctor found anything yet?"

David picked up a stapled packet of papers from his desk. "The report I got said that Dr. McAdam hasn't found anything physically wrong with her yet. He's been monitoring her own healing rate and keeping track of what she's doing to herself while she's asleep. She's still making some small adjustments but nothing too major, it looks like."

Before Marc could ask any more questions, the phone on David's desk started to ring. He picked it up, mildly irritated at the interruption, but his attitude swiftly changed. "That's great news, thanks for calling. Yes, we're on our way right now."

He hung up the phone and looked over at the other two men as he stood up and reached for his jacket. "That was the hospital. Jen just woke up."

Marc grinned for the first time since Jen had been taken. "It's about damn time," he said as he headed for the door. "A nap's one thing but this is pushing it a little."

Even Charlie snickered as they stepped into the elevator. "I wouldn't recommend saying that in front of her," he said. "From what I've heard, she's liable to beat you with one of the flower arrangements her sister brought down for her."

Marc thought about that. "You've got a point," he conceded and looked at David. "Do we have time for me to grab my body armor before we go?"

Chapter 2

Monitors flashed zigzags of green and yellow light. Quiet beeping sounds filled her head with a steady staccato of noise. Jen looked down at herself and noticed that she was covered in a thick white sheet and there was an intravenous drip attached to her right arm. Further away, she could hear people talking, their voices muted as though they were trying to be quiet and she could hear someone breathing nearby. Jen turned her head to see who was talking and to try and figure out where she was.

The room was dark, although not quite as dark as the room she had lived in for the last month or so had been. Small bits of light shone into the room from under the door, from the lighted machines, and from beneath the heavy curtains that covered the windows. A man sat in the shadows, slumped in a chair and snoring softly. As she moved her head to the side in order to get a better look around her, another monitor joined in the chorus of noise and a small green light began to flash. Not sure what that meant, Jen lay back in the position she had woken in and closed her eyes, feigning sleep. Until she was able to figure out what fresh flavor of hell she was in now, she would rather not alert anyone to the fact that she was awake.

The door opened only seconds later. Jen could tell that there were bright lights just outside her room by the glare that shone over her face and penetrated her eyelids. A large figure stepped into the room, evidenced by the shadow as it moved across the glare. Jen opened her eyes the tiniest fraction and peered through her eyelashes, trying to remain as still as she could while feigning sleep and still being able to see what was going on. She'd had enough of being blindsided with surprises, so she had no intention of ignoring whatever was about to happen to her until it was too late.

The sleeping man in the chair jumped to

his feet, stepping to face the person who had opened the door. Blinded by the brightness of the lights shining in from the hallway outside, Jen couldn't see who either of the people was.

"Calm down," one of them said in a voice Jen didn't recognize. "It's just me. One of the monitors recorded a change in her readings, so I'm just here to make sure she's still okay." As he spoke, Jen realized that the voice was coming from the man who had just entered the room. As the other man backed down, Jen thought the shape of his outline looked familiar but she couldn't see well enough to be sure.

The man who had spoken stepped quietly to her bedside. As her vision adjusted to the change in lighting, she noted that he was dressed in black pants and a white lab coat and smelled slightly of disinfectant. Although she was curious to see more of him, she couldn't risk turning her head to look more directly at the newcomer without giving herself away.

The other man stepped closer to her as well and once he moved into the light, Jen recognized him. He was about six feet tall, with shaggy brown hair and what appeared to be a few weeks' growth of facial hair. His clothes looked as though this wasn't the first time they had been slept in and Jen had never expected to be so happy to see him. "Troy?" Troy Franklin was her roommate, friend, and part-time bodyguard.

He stepped closer to her bedside, reaching down to take her hand as he did. "Jen? Are you awake?"

She opened her eyes further, still uncertain about the stranger in the room but trusting that Troy wouldn't let anything bad happen to her. "Where am I?" Her voice was faint, even to her own ears, and her throat was dry and scratchy. She reached up to brush a lock of her hair out of her face. The hair was almost black and had grown out far enough to get in her eyes again.

While the stranger checked her machines and made notes on a clipboard, Troy explained. "You're in North Bank Hospital, so you're safe, okay? You collapsed during the last mission and we brought you in here to be taken care of."

Jen blinked at him in confusion. She hadn't been out on any missions lately, at least not that she could remember. The expression on

Troy's face caused her to keep quiet about it, at least for the moment. "How long have I been in here?"

"Six days," he explained. "They think that you had too much exposure to the energy in the dark plane, so they're trying to get that cleaned out." He looked over at the man in the lab coat before continuing. "You were pretty beat up, too, so they needed to get you put back together."

"But it looks like you're doing pretty well," the stranger said as he set her chart down and stepped closer to her. "All of your vitals have gone down to normal levels, so that's a good sign." He was taller than Troy, with broad shoulders and sandy blond hair that showed a hint of curl even with the short style it was in.

"My name is Dr. Greg McAdam; I was called in to oversee your case." He smiled down at Jen as he spoke. "We'd been wondering how long you were going to be unconscious, and I know a lot of your friends have been pretty worried about you."

She looked from the doctor to Troy, who nodded at her reassuringly. "There's been someone here with you constantly since you were brought in. We've been taking shifts."

As her eyes and her mind cleared, Jen realized that there was something unusual about her new doctor. He had energy around him, similar to the energy the demons had used but not quite the same. As he listened to her heart and her lungs through his stethoscope, she could feel his energy change, as though he was directing it while he examined her.

Fear shot through her body at the idea that this might be another demonic trap and she reached up to push him off of her. "What are you doing?"

He stepped back and raised both of his hands, showing the stethoscope. "I'm just listening to you, making sure that everything's working the way it's supposed to."

She shook her head. "No. Get away from me." She struggled to sit up and scoot herself backwards on the bed, determined to increase the distance between herself and the demon claiming to be a doctor. To her dismay, the week she had spent unconscious in the bed had left her far weaker than she normally would have been. Rather than pushing herself backwards, away from the monster posing as a doctor, she only managed to lean away from him, slumping against the side of the bed closest to Troy.

Her friend stepped closer, trying to calm her down. "It's okay, you're safe." Before he touched her, however, he stopped and stepped back. "Oh, shit," he muttered. He turned back towards the demon in the white coat. "Could you give us a minute?"

"Take as long as you need," he said as he walked towards the door.

Once he was gone, Troy sat on the edge of the bed and looked at Jen. "I know what they did to you," he explained. "Would you rather I have a woman come in to be with you? I've heard that it's easier to deal with a woman at first."

Jen blinked at him in confusion. "What are you talking about?"

Now it was Troy's turn to be confused. "Before Todd was able to break through the barrier, we could see through it, so we knew what was happening to you over there. The doctors said you might have some memory loss. Do you remember any of it?"

"I remember all of it but that has nothing to do with the demon that was just here."

"He's not a demon," Troy tried to explain. "He's a doctor that the NPIB sent in, a specialist to help take care of you."

Jen shook her head. "He has energy all around him and he was moving it just like the demons did."

"Okay, I think I understand." He reached forward and carefully took her hand. When she didn't flinch, he smiled at her. "Todd said that you had been absorbing energy while you were over there, so I think I get it. But Greg's not a demon, he's a psychic. He uses his energy to heal people, not to hurt them."

"He's a psychic?" she asked in confusion as she looked towards the door where the man had left. "I thought you said he was a doctor."

"He's both. He uses whichever he needs to when he's trying to heal someone. So when he was using his energy, he was probably just using it to make sure you were actually okay."

Jen thought about it and decided it made sense. Troy wouldn't have let a demon anywhere near her and he sure wouldn't have defended one. "Damn, I'm sorry," she said.

"Don't be sorry, I'm sure he understands. You've been through a lot." He stood as though he was going to go get the doctor again, but Jen called him back.

"Why did you say that I'd been hurt when we were out on mission?"

"Because nobody's been told that you were a captive over there too," he explained. "Todd thought it'd be better for everyone to be focused on making you better instead of worrying about the possibility of you being infected by the darkness."

"So nobody knows?"

"A few people know, mostly just the people that were there when we came to get you. You know as well as I do that all of them can be trusted to keep their mouths shut, so you don't have to worry about anything, just work on getting better."

"Do you know if anyone ran a disease screening and stuff on me?" Jen asked. It was a reasonable question, considering that there was a large battery of tests that were done to make sure that there wouldn't be any long-term, lasting effects from blood transfer during her recent extended assault. However, since none of the medical staff seemed to know how extensive that assault on her had been, there was no reason to run any of them.

"Joel talked one of his friends into running the tests under a different name, so nobody knew that anything unusual was being done with yours. But you don't have to worry, everything came up clean. No disease, no infections, nothing."

Joel Peters was one of Jen's closest friends. He happened to work at North Bank Hospital as a volunteer, so it was no surprise that he would have a friend or two that he could ask for help when he needed something. Not only was Jen relieved to hear that all of her tests had come back negative, but she was also happy to hear that Joel was okay too.

When Jen had been captured, her entire team had been captivated by a demoness. She had used her mental dominance power to force all of the men on the team, plus Joel and Troy who had been there as well, to do her bidding. Jen knew that of all the men that had been there that day, Joel had to have been taking what had happened the hardest. Before Jen had been turned over to the demon who had held her for the last month, the demoness had ordered Joel to kill her. Jen could still clearly see the edge of the blade as it swung down towards her as one of her closest and dearest friends attempted to cut her still-beating heart from her body.

Once she had calmed down, Troy went over to the door and signaled for Dr. McAdam to come back in. The doctor walked slowly, being careful to keep his hands where Jen could see them, until Jen sighed at him. "You can stop that, you know."

He put his hands down and walked closer to her. "I didn't want to scare you again, so I figured I'd take it easy." He pulled his stethoscope out of a pocket. "Are you okay now?"

Jen nodded and relaxed. "Troy just told me you were a psychic." She smiled wryly. "I thought you were another demon, just pretending to be a doctor."

Dr. McAdam looked at her in surprise and chuckled. "No, I'm not a demon. But I thought there was something unusual when I was listening to you, so I wanted to check and make sure it wasn't something that I needed to fix quickly. I hadn't meant to startle you."

Once he was finished his examination, Jen asked, "So how bad is it?"

"Not bad at all," he answered, smiling at her reassuringly. His teeth were almost unnaturally straight, and she wondered briefly what kind of whitener he used to make them so bright. "Everything seems to have healed nicely, so there doesn't seem to be much to worry about there."

He hooked her chart at the foot of her bed and walked out of the room for a moment, returning with a small paper cup that was half filled with water. "Take a drink," he said as he held it out to her. "I'll go have something sent up for you to eat and if you can hold everything down all right, we should be able to take the IV out soon." She took a sip of the cool water, still trying to get herself back under control.

As she sipped at the water, Dr. McAdam left again. As soon as he was gone, Jen lowered the cup and turned to Troy again. "What about the other prisoners? Did you get them all out?"

"Yeah. They're all safe and sound, so all you have to worry about right now is resting and getting your strength back up."

They sat in silence while she drank her slowly warming water. Soon, Dr. McAdam returned with a plate for her, although Jen wasn't sure that she agreed with his assertion that the stuff on it was food. She recognized scrambled eggs but the grayish mass of goop was unidentifiable.

"Vegetable paste," he provided when she looked over at him doubtfully. "I think its carrots, peas, and some sort of bean; I'm not exactly positive which."

As she poked at the food, Dr. McAdam looked thoughtfully between Jen and Troy. "Just out of curiosity," he said, "when are you planning to start telling me the truth?"

Jen almost choked at the bite of rubbery egg she had just shoved into her mouth. Her eyes darted from Dr. McAdam to Troy and back to the doctor again. "The truth about what?" she asked finally.

"About what really happened to you?"

"We already told you," Troy answered. "She

got hurt when we were out rescuing the hostages from the demon's lair." He stood up and walked closer to the doctor. Troy was a hybrid, half human and half werewolf and he never passed up an opportunity to use that fact to his advantage.

Surprisingly, the doctor refused to back down from the hybrid's intimidation tactic. "I know what you told me," he responded, keeping his voice level and meeting Troy's eyes squarely. "What I want to know is what really happened."

Jen looked back and forth between the two men doubtfully. Although she knew that it was important to be honest with her doctor, she wondered if there was a reason that Troy had lied about her captivity.

When it became obvious that neither of them was going to answer, Dr. McAdam sighed. He reached behind him and closed the door, effectively blocking out the rest of the hospital. "Confidentiality between a doctor and a patient isn't just a myth," he explained to Jen. "Anything you tell me will stay with me and it could help me in my treatment program for you." He looked back toward Troy. "And I understand that you want to help your friend, it's obvious that she's been through a lot. But it's also obvious that she's been through a lot more than just what you and your friends have been telling me."

Jen sighed and looked down at her food. She poked at the mystery paste for a moment as she thought. "I didn't get hurt on the rescue mission," she admitted finally. "I wasn't even on the mission."

Dr. McAdam stepped forward and took a seat in the chair that Troy hadn't been using. "I suspected as much. What else can you tell me?"

Jen poked at her food some more as she felt tears well up in her eyes again. "I *was* the rescue mission." She reached out and took the fresh cup of water that had been brought in with her meal and took a drink of it before continuing. "They were there to rescue me."

"I was captured by the demons and taken to their plane. That's where..." her voice broke and she couldn't finish the sentence.

Dr. McAdam reached out and took her hand. "I know. I saw some of the damage while you were healing from it, so you don't need to explain to me exactly what happened if you don't want to, okay?"

Jen wiped the tears from her face without looking up. "That's why I thought you were a demon," she explained, her voice still weak and shaky with emotion. "Your energy felt a lot like theirs."

He blinked at her in surprise. "You can feel the energy flow?" he asked. "There wasn't any mention of that in your chart."

"There wouldn't have been; I learned how to feel it while I was over there."

He nodded understandingly and asked her a few more questions before reassuring her again that nothing she had said would be shared with anyone. "Since this is so important to you, I won't add it in any of my reports, either." When she smiled her thanks at him, he smiled back at her and headed out.

Shortly after she finished her so-called meal, Jen drifted off to sleep again. When she woke, Troy was gone but there was a woman sitting in the chair that he had occupied. Her hair was a riot of curls, most of which were brown but a few still held shades of blue, purple, and red where her last batch of dye hadn't completely washed out. She was smaller than Jen and dressed in frayed blue jeans, silver shoes, and a short-sleeved shirt with a picture of a reindeer lined up in the center of a set of crosshairs. "Give me the good stuff," the shirt demanded, "Or kiss your reindeer goodbye."

She was reading a novel, angled in her seat to catch the meager light that shone in from the hallway. Even in the dim light, Jen could easily identify her best friend. "Hey, Sahara."

Sahara Peters looked over at her and set the book down on a small table that sat nearby. "Hey yourself," she answered. "How're you feeling?"

"Not too bad," Jen answered. "Tired, a little groggy, and kind of anxious to get out of here but a hell of a lot better than I was *before* I got here."

"I guess it's a good thing I brought you one of these then, isn't it?" She reached over to the table she had set her book on and picked up a tall brown paper cup with a plastic lid and the logo of Beene Brothers, Jen's favorite coffee shop. "Four shots of white mocha good-ness and one shot of coconut," she explained as she handed it over. "Guaranteed to cure that grogginess."

Jen accepted the cup greedily. This would be the first caffeine she'd gotten since before her capture and she eagerly took the first sip, not caring in the slightest that the beverage didn't even pretend to be hot anymore. "Mmm," she sighed. "I needed that."

"It looked like you did. Troy called me after you woke up. I'd have been here sooner, but he said you went back to sleep and not to bother yet." She smiled over at her friend. "I know how much you like to sleep but isn't a week enough?"

Jen had to snicker as she took another drink of her coffee. "I'm surprised they let you bring this in; I wouldn't have expected coffee to be on my list of allowed foods until after they got this thing out," she said as she lifted her arm.

"It's not," Sahara admitted. "That's *my* cof-fee, of course."

Jen slowly felt the sleepiness subside as they sat and talked. Sahara explained about how anxious everyone had been while she was gone, and how relieved everyone was to hear that she was back.

"Patrick and his crew have spent the last few days getting the last of your stuff packed up and moved to the new house. Apparently, they hadn't wanted to move anything until they got you back." Jen had completely forgotten about the fire that had severely damaged her home before her capture. She had finalized the purchase of a new home only days before the demons had taken her.

She explained about how everyone at Sugar and Spice, Sahara's herbal shop, had been pulling for her while she was gone. "A lot of them wanted to go out and get you back themselves. They probably would have, too, if they'd known where you were."

They were still talking when David, Marc and someone that Jen didn't recognize walked into the room. Jen was happy to see both her boss and her unit leader but she was curious and more than a little hesitant about the third man, who wore a grey suit and red tie. He seemed familiar for some reason but she couldn't place where she had seen him.

David and Marc came over to hug her, both of them grinning broadly. Once each of them had been able to greet her, David introduced her to the third man. "Jen, this is Charlie Winters. He's with the NPIB and he's been helping us get you back," he explained. "There are other NPIB agents waiting to talk to you also, but Todd's been doing a pretty good job of keeping them away from you."

Jen continued eyeing Charlie. "You look familiar. Where have I seen you before?"

"I was with the team when they went to rescue you."

That explained why she couldn't immediately recognize where she had seen him. "So you know what happened?" She looked over at David uncertainly. "I thought nobody knew about that."

"I've agreed to keep the specifics out of my reports," Charlie responded, "so there shouldn't be too much flack over everything that happened to you."

"But you're NPIB," she said. "Aren't you guys

all supposed to be researching this kind of thing and all that?" She eyed him suspiciously. "Or is that what you're doing here?"

He shook his head. "I'm not here to research anything. I'm just here to make sure that you're all right." He smiled down at her. "And, I have to say, it's a pleasure to finally meet you in person."

Jen nodded, not sure whether meeting Charlie was a good thing or a bad one. Rather than dwell on it, however, she turned to David again. "What about the other people that were held over there? Troy said you got everyone out. Are they all okay?"

"Yes," David agreed, "thanks to you. Some are still being treated for their injuries but most of them have been released and sent to a group home where they can be treated further, both physically and emotionally. A therapist has been assigned to them to help them work through everything that they went through."

He looked down at her thoughtfully. "There's one assigned to you, too; there isn't any way to deny that you've been through a pretty traumatic time lately. That's not something you have to worry about right now but the sooner you start working through what happened to you, the better off you'll be."

Jen shook her head. "I'm fine. I have a gun and a smuggled cup of coffee and that's all the therapy I need." She grinned up at her boss, but then the grin fell to a sigh when it wasn't returned. "I'm really fine. I made it through, I survived and Cylin's dead, so I really couldn't ask for more. Right now, all I want is about a gallon of coffee and some clothes so I can go home."

"Cylin?" Charlie asked. "Was that the demon's name?"

She nodded. "I don't think they realized that I caught them referring to each other by name."

David blinked at her in surprise. "Them? There was only one there when we showed up."

"Apparently there were three. Cylin was the sadistic bastard you guys took out; he was the one that enjoyed beating on everyone. I'm not sure where Thaxter was, he wasn't there all the time. The third one's a female named Vanitha, she's the one that the team met. I never actually saw her in Derathim but I overheard them talking about how she was captured." She looked between the men questioningly. "Was it us? Did we get her?"

"We have the one that caught you in custody right now, she's been in the basement the whole time you were gone."

Jen smiled at that, less in amusement and more in anticipation. "Good. Because as soon as I get out of here, I'm going to kick the crap out of that bitch."

Charlie snickered at that, but David shook his head. "No, she's going to be transferred to a more secure location before you get out of here. It appears that demonic blood can be used to help nullify the demon's powers over humans, so the NPIB wants to see how effective it can be against other things, too."

Jen wasn't sure what she thought of that idea. "On the one hand, I want to get her blood for you myself but I'm not sure I like the idea of experimenting on her. Isn't there some other way of doing it?"

Charlie shook his head. "It's not our decision to make. As soon as the guys upstairs heard we had access to a demon, they demanded their crack at her." At her expression of doubt, he shrugged. "It's out of my hands."

"Speaking of getting out of here," Jen changed the subject, "do you have any idea how much longer it's going to be?"

"That's up to Greg," Charlie said. "But I'll ask him." He turned and headed out the door.

"I should get going, too," David added. "You still need your rest." He followed the taller man out into the hallway.

She spent three more days in the hospital, where the doctor and his team ran countless tests on her and checked all of her monitors constantly to make sure she was actually healthy enough to go home. A few times, she heard Todd out in the hallway arguing with people, but he never explained what any of the arguments had been about. All he would say was that she would find out soon enough and not to worry before she had to.

Todd was her twin brother and she loved him dearly. However, there were times when he could be overprotective and, given the current situation, she couldn't really blame him for his caution. She was still curious about who he was arguing with and why, but she wasn't going to press the matter right then.

With nothing better to do, she flipped on the television and scrolled through channels. Against her better judgment, she stopped on a news channel, which showed a group of protesters from an anti-paranormal group who were marching on a city hall just a handful of cities away. "Protesters are calling for the re-illegalization of all vampires and werewolves," the newscaster explained. "They have been marching on every state capital and city hall for the last six weeks, targeting a different city every week. What started as a small movement has grown over these weeks, and the force is now hundreds of men, women and children."

Other people, apparently those who sympathized with the vampires and werewolves who were being targeted by the protesters, had gathered as well. They formed a united front against the rallying group, ensuring that the protesters stayed in one tight group, closely packed together. Jen wondered how many of them were humans and how many were werewolves and hybrids. Since the footage showed that the rally was during the daytime, she doubted there were any vampires in the crowd.

Quickly bored with the news, she flipped through the meager stations that the hospital got. "Why aren't there any good cartoons?" she moaned as she landed on yet another soap opera. "Who watches this crap, anyway?" Bored out of her mind, she was pleased for the interruption when the rest of her team stopped by to see her.

J.J. Monroe, her closest friend on the team, was the first to arrive. The tall blonde walked into the room, uncontested by Todd, and handed her a small bouquet of multicolored daisies. "I looked at the flowers they had in the gift shop, but you didn't really seem the pink rose type," he explained.

Jen grinned at him and accepted the bouquet. She sniffed at the flowers, grimacing at their fragrance. "They made them prettier but it's too bad they couldn't make them smell any better."

J.J. chuckled at her response and took the flowers back. He set them onto the counter where she could still see them and sank into a chair. "Yep, it definitely looks like you're doing better."

Mike Brown, whose goatee had started to grow long again, was the next to arrive. He had decided to forego flowers and had decided on balloons instead. Jen could tell that he had gotten his from the hospital gift shop because half of them said "Get Well Soon" and the other half said "Congratulations on Your New Baby!"

He was followed by Ty Williams, a tall man with midnight skin and eyes. His head looked freshly shaved and he handed her the largest stuffed octopus she had ever seen. "It was going to be a teddy bear," he explained, "but I had the kids last weekend and we went to the aquarium. I saw that and knew it was perfect."

Jen couldn't hold the laughter any longer. "You guys are awesome," she giggled.

The trio stayed for most of the afternoon until Dr. McAdam arrived and asked them to leave so that he could give Jen another checkup. Her IV had been removed already, once she had proven she could hold solid foods down, but she still wasn't allowed to have more than one person in her room for long periods of time.

"You're getting better," Dr. McAdam admitted, "but you still need rest, you need time to heal." He made a couple notes in her chart. "But the good news is that all of your tests are continuing to come back negative, so it looks like we'll be able to release you by tomorrow afternoon at the latest."

Jen smiled in relief at the news but before Dr. McAdam could explain any more, there was a commotion outside her room. "I'm sure everything's fine," he reassured her as his eyes darted toward the sound, "but I'd better go check." He headed out the door, and Jen wondered what was happening. She knew that there had been someone guarding her room the whole time she had been there and worried that the commotion involved whoever was watching her now.

After only seconds, she decided that she didn't feel like being a sitting duck. Slowly, she crept over to her door and opened it just a crack to peek outside. Ty was standing in front of the door, but he didn't appear to be engaged in the commotion. Because of that, Jen felt a bit more secure and opened the door further. A man was on a gurney in the hallway, bound but still thrashing against his restraints. As Jen watched, he reached his head to the side and snapped at a doctor who was trying to tend to him. His sharp fangs barely missed their target and Jen whistled under her breath. "It's still daylight," she muttered. "What's a vamp doing out right now?"

Ty looked down at her and tried to push her back into the room but Jen wasn't moving. "He's restrained, calm down," she explained. "What happened?"

Ty shrugged and stepped aside so that she could see more clearly. "Sounds like he slipped into a blood rage while he was at home. His wife called it in."

Jen's heart sank at his words. "Did he kill her?"

Ty shook his head. "One of the nurses said that he locked himself in a bathroom so that she could call for help. Pretty clear thinking, I'd say."

"No kidding. I thought they lose all control when they snap."

Ty shrugged. "He's still fighting it, looks like.

The paramedics gave him a huge dose of tranquilizers but he's still pretty active."

"Why don't they give him more?"

"Can't," he explained. "There's only a certain amount you can give a vamp before it starts to do permanent damage to them. If they get overdosed on tranquillizers, they might not be able to come back out of rage." He pointed to a crying woman that was following the gurney down the hall. "Guessing that's the wife."

She stood a few paces back from the action, looking between the doctors as they tried to stabilize the vampire. As far as Jen could see, she was unharmed but scared. "He's really not violent," she insisted. "He's registered and everything, he was even just at a blood bank yesterday so there's no reason for him to be starving."

"There have been a lot more lately," Ty said down to Jen. "Vamps have been raging all over the place. We were sent out after a few while you were gone. Nobody's sure what's causing it, though."

"So this is happening a lot?" she asked blankly.

"Mostly class one and two vamps but yeah. They've been losing control and biting people, but most of 'em were pretty tame before they lost it. The first ones were put down pretty quickly, but that was before we realized there was something causing it. A lot of people have been looking pretty closely at them, trying to figure out what the trigger is."

Jen looked at him thoughtfully. "And they still don't know what's behind it?"

"Everyone has their own ideas," Ty shrugged. "Some people think that there isn't anything unusual at all, that they're natural predators and this is what they do but that's the minority opinion. Most people think that there's got to be something causing it.

"Personally, I wonder if it has anything to do with the increasing levels of dark energy that are being reported all over the place."

Wondering at this idea, Jen looked more closely at the vampire as he was pushed past her room and towards another room further down the hall. She could sense a lot of dark energy swirling around him and recognized that it felt much more like the energy that the demons had used. She could also feel Dr. McAdam's energy as he tried to counteract whatever was ailing the vampire. "I think I have an idea," she said as she pushed further past Ty into the hall. "But I need to get closer."

She had already expelled all of the energy that she had stolen from the demons, so she knew that taking a little from the vampire wouldn't hurt her. If Ty's theory was right, it might end up doing a lot of good and she might be able to help the vampire, not to mention his terrified wife.

"What are you doing?" Ty asked as she pushed past him. "Are you crazy?"

"Only a little," she answered as she stepped further into the hall. She headed for the room that the vampire was taken into and peered inside. There were too many people inside for her to get a clear view of the vampire, but she could feel its energy more strongly in the con-centrated area. She took a step backwards and looked over at Ty. "Catch me if I fall, okay? This tends to make me a little dizzy." She turned back to the vampire again. "Now, let's see if I can do this here, too."

She closed her eyes and focused on the energy, following the swirling pattern it made in the air. Slowly, she drew the energy outward. As it moved, she was able to redirect it further and pull more of the darkness away from the vampire and into herself. She could hear Ty asking what she was doing but she ignored him. There wasn't any good way to explain what she was trying to do, or how she knew she could and didn't want to spend the energy at that moment talking. She had more important things to do.

She could still feel the vampire's rage, unsubdued at her attempt. As she opened her eyes, she discovered that Dr. McAdam had looked up from the vampire and was looking directly at her. As she drew more energy out of the room, he started to move towards the door. When he got too close, his energy began to flow into the path the dark energy was taking and Jen had to stop drawing it altogether.

"I think it'd be best if you went back to your room," the psychic doctor said to her, a strange expression on his face. "I'll be in soon to check on you. Just let me finish in here first."

Without waiting for an answer, Ty took her

by the arm and led her down the hall. As they went, Jen realized that it probably hadn't been the smartest idea to draw that much energy in front of a psychic.

Chapter 3

When she was finally released from the hospital, Marc helped her pack all of her stuff into his truck and gave her a ride home. It had been a while since she had seen her new house and having all of her belongings there made it seem even stranger than it would have been if she had gone home to her old house. She wandered through the living room, checking out the few pieces of new furniture that Patrick had picked up in her absence. Both he and Troy had set up their belongings in the spare room, so at least the living room wasn't cluttered with their suitcases and duffel bags. Even Patrick's air mattress was gone.

She headed upstairs to see how much work there was left to do in her bedroom, where she discovered that someone had made her bed and put all of her clothes away. In the attached bathroom, she discovered towels already hanging on the rack, ready to be used. All of her toiletries were put away where she could find them, which led her to believe that Todd had been responsible for that part of the unpacking.

Marc walked with her through the house, checking to be sure that each room was empty before letting her enter. As annoyed as she was by the excessive attention, all she really wanted was to jump into the shower and wash the stink of the hospital out of her skin. She knew that it was more of a mental response than an actual smell but she wanted it gone anyway.

Before she was even able to start the water, however, the doorbell rang. She looked out of one of the windows in the upstairs hall and saw a black car parked in her driveway. With a sigh, she headed downstairs to see who it was.

Marc was at the door, arguing with the four men who stood on her doorstep. All four of them wore black suits and none of them looked overly friendly. As Marc blocked the door, the two in front opened their badges and showed them to him. Looking none too pleased, Marc turned towards Jen.

"These guys are from the NPIB. This is Agent Thompson," he indicated the blond man, "and Agent Brooks. They're pretty insistent that they need to talk to you."

"Can this wait? I was about to get in the shower."

"No, I'm afraid it can't," the blonde answered. "We've been waiting to talk to you for far too long already."

"Look," she sighed. "I've been away for a little while and I've been home for all of fifteen minutes..."

She would have said more but Agent Thompson interrupted her. "We understand that, but we do need to talk with you. Your brother has refused to speak with us at all and there are many things that we need to clear up." He set his mouth in a firm line. "Today."

There were a great many things that Jen was willing to overlook. There were also a lot of things that she disliked but being interrupted was one thing that irritated her more than almost anything else. She leaned against the door jamb and crossed her arms, eyebrows lowered. "So what do you want?"

"We would like you to come with us," he explained. "We need to have a couple of assessments done and they are much easier to do back at our office."

"Beyond that, we have a few questions for you," Agent Brooks added.

"I don't think so," Jen responded. "As I just said, I just got home and I'm not in the mood to go anywhere right now." She looked between the two agents. "If you have questions for me, you can ask them here. Other than that, it can wait."

Jen looked over at Marc but decided not to say anything to him in front of the NPIB agents. She wasn't sure exactly why, but he didn't appear to trust them. Beyond that, they had said that her brother hadn't been willing to talk with them, which was all the indication she needed to know not to blindly believe whatever they had to say. Whether they meant Todd or Patrick didn't matter. If her brothers didn't trust them, she didn't either.

Instead, she looked over at the agents that

had identified themselves. "What all did you want to talk to me about?" She looked between them and beyond them at the two who hadn't spoken yet. "And what kind of tests?"

"First of all," Agent Thompson explained, "We need to assess your magical and psychic skills. Beyond that, we need to check the level of tainting from your exposure to Derathim."

"I've already been assessed," Jen asserted. "Years ago, but it's still on record. Go check it and come back to bother me when you have real questions."

"We're aware of your test results," Agent Brooks said. "However, those tests were performed many years ago and recent events have led us to question their validity."

"Maybe we should step inside and discuss this where it's a bit warmer," Marc interrupted, gesturing out to the light snow that was falling. "There's no reason to stand in the doorway and argue about it."

Jen sighed and stepped away from the door jamb. "Fine," she said and turned to step inside. The men followed her in and everyone gathered in the living room. Once everyone was inside,

Marc closed the door and turned back to the group.

"First of all," he said to Jen, "you should know that you aren't required to answer any of their questions if you aren't comfortable with them. They aren't here with a court order, so you can refuse to answer anything you want to and nothing will happen."

When Jen nodded, he turned to the men, who looked much less pleased about what he had to say. "Furthermore, you are now inside her private residence. If for no other reason than that, there will be no casting while you are here, other than the magical and psychic assessment you guys mentioned earlier. Understood?"

The four men looked among themselves for a moment before the blond agent scowled his assent. "Understood. However, we will also be testing for darkness taint." He smiled over at Marc, with a thin, tight-lipped smirk. "I'm sure I don't have to remind you how dangerous those who have been tainted by the dark plane can become and there is no doubt that Ms. Rice has been to the dark plane."

"Fine, but that's it. Anything else you want,

any other tests you want to run or if you want to try and take Jen anywhere, you can get a court order. Until then, the rules stand."

None of the visiting men looked pleased at the arrangement but it was the closest they had been to Jen since they were sent out after her, so they had no choice but to agree. Since the only places to sit in the living room were the new couch or on Troy's Bark-O-Lounger, Jen headed for the kitchen to have a seat at the dining room table. She figured that if she was going to have to endure these irritating men for very long, she wasn't going to do it very far from her coffeepot.

"First of all," Agent Brooks explained to Jen, "you should be aware that we aren't buying the official story of where you've been lately and what you've been up to. We know that you weren't a member of the rescue team that went to Derathim to rescue the hostages that were being held there."

"What makes you say that?" she asked as she pulled her favorite coffee cup out of the cupboard. It was one that her brother Todd had given her almost a year before, with a motto on the side that read "*Instant Human, Just Add Coffee.*" The saying wasn't simply humorous, it was highly accurate. Jen simply didn't function without dangerously high levels of caffeine in her system.

"For one, you were missing for quite some time before the retrieval mission. Beyond, that, the other people who were retrieved in that mission have said that you were imprisoned with them for a while." He looked at her, waiting for a response.

When Jen simply looked back at him blankly, his eyebrows lowered and he leaned on his elbows towards her across the table. "Do you intend to respond?"

Jen looked up at him in surprise. "Respond to what? You said you had questions, so I'm waiting."

"That *was* a question and we'd appreciate an answer."

Jen shook her head. "No it wasn't, it was a statement." She took a drink of her coffee and smiled at them. "There is a difference, according to my last English teacher."

Both men looked at her dumbfounded for a

long moment. Finally Agent Brooks asked, "In that case, where were you during the time you were missing?"

"I don't think that's something I want to discuss right now," she answered. "Maybe we can talk about it later but not right now."

"Fine. How would you explain the accelerated healing rate that you displayed while you were still in the hospital?"

She shrugged at that one. "I'd guess that you should ask the doctors that treated me about that one, I was asleep the whole time." She looked between them again. "But it might have had something to do with the psychic doctor that was treating me. That would probably account for a lot of it."

They continued to press her for more information about where she had been, what she had been doing, and how she got the healing ability that she showed in the hospital. Most of the questions were ones that she either couldn't explain or wasn't ready to talk about but when she had the familiar feeling of magic being cast on her, she called a halt to the proceedings.

"I thought we had an agreement," she said

as she pushed her chair back and rose to her feet. "I was willing to let you into my home, a home that you have now spent almost as much time in as I have and all you had to do was keep your mage from casting on me." She turned and glared at one of the men who hadn't spoken but who still stank of magical skill. "Had I realized you had no intention of honoring that arrangement, I wouldn't have bothered." She stepped away from the table. "I'm sure you can manage to show yourselves out without causing any more problems."

Both of the men who had been talking fell silent. "So it's true then," Agent Thompson commented. "You really can feel it." They smiled at each other. "Sounds like you have a bit more going on than we had thought. We had just been under the impression that all you could do was to heal yourself but if you can feel when spells are cast on you, that might be indicative of an additional power that we hadn't been aware of."

She turned and glared at the one who had spoken. "My twin brother is a fairly powerful mage. I've known what it felt like for magic to be cast on me since I was twelve. There's nothing surprising about that."

"My fault," the mage spoke up for the first time. "I should have warned you but I hadn't been aware that you were so closely related to a mage."

"That doesn't matter," Jen answered, still incensed. "You weren't supposed to cast anything."

"True," the mage agreed, "I'm not supposed to cast anything except for the magical skill assessment, which is what I was doing."

Jen evaluated the man, not sure how much she trusted him. While she knew when a spell was cast on her, she couldn't always tell what that spell had been, so it was entirely possible that the mage was telling the truth. "Fine," she relented. She went to sit down again but decided to pour herself a fresh cup of coffee before retaking her seat. "Go ahead and do your assessments but that'd better be all you do." She sent the mage one more warning glare before taking a drink of her coffee.

Everyone remained quiet while the mage murmured his incantation, waiting for a signal from him that it was finished. Aware of what the first spell had felt like, Jen focused on his magical energy as he cast his second spell, trying to detect any change from the first one. When he was finished, however, she had to admit that the second casting hadn't felt any different than the first one. Because of that, she was willing to admit that he was probably only casting what he was supposed to.

Both of the agents looked closely at the mage as he finished his spell. Before answering the agents' silent questions, he turned to Jen. "Could I have a drink of water, please?"

She leveled her gaze on him for a moment before standing again to get one of the bottles of water from the fridge. "Trust me, you don't want to drink the water out of the tap," she explained as she handed the bottle over.

He accepted it gratefully and took a long drink before recapping it and turning to the agents again. "She's not registering any power," he explained. "Kind of unusual for having a mage as a twin, one would expect to find something, even something very mild. But she shows nothing, neither light nor dark."

Both of the agents appeared taken aback by this. "Nothing?" Agent Thompson finally asked. "Are you sure?" When the mage simply shrugged, he turned to the other man, who Jen could only assume was a psychic. His energy felt much like Dr. McAdam's had in the hospital and the agents had said that they intended to test her for both magical and psychic, so they would need a psychic to test her.

Jen could sense his energy as it moved around her, but it felt strange. It wasn't as dark as the demonic energy had been, nor was it as light as Dr. McAdam's. She tried to stay still as the psychic performed his examination, suppressing the urge to absorb the energy that he was putting around her. She watched the expression on his face change from smug superiority to one of almost disbelief. As his energy retreated, Jen let out a sigh of relief.

"Well?" Agent Brooks asked as the psychic sat back. "What is she hiding?"

The psychic shook his head. "Nothing," he said finally. "She's completely blank."

Jen looked at the man in surprise. He had to have noticed something unusual and she wondered why he hadn't said anything. Luckily, she caught herself before she opened her mouth to ask him about it.

Agent Thompson became even more irritated at the psychic's findings. He looked between the mage and the psychic, his face becoming ruddier with every breath he took. "She has to have something," he snarled at them. "She was in the dark plane for a month, so there should at least be something there from that."

Both of the men shook their heads. "I wasn't able to detect any taint," the psychic pointed out. "If I had, I would have said as much."

"Fine," the agent growled and turned to the mage. "What about you? There has to be something more that you didn't see; you know as well as I do that she should be registering with something, *anything*. What did you miss?"

The mage blinked calmly at the irate man. "I didn't miss anything," he replied, "because there was nothing there to miss. She was completely open and unguarded, so she wasn't hiding anything. There simply wasn't any taint of darkness there."

"Are you satisfied?" Jen interrupted the

argument. When everyone turned towards her again, she gave them her sweetest smile. "I've had a rough week or three and I would really like to go get my shower and take a nap. If you don't have anything else you'd like to ask me about, I believe it's time for you to go."

"No," Agent Thompson barked at her. "We still have more questions for you and I expect you to answer them honestly. Where were you?"

"Upstairs," she answered. "And I have every intention of returning there." She put her cup in the sink and headed for the doorway.

"We aren't finished talking to you," Agent Thompson said as he stood and moved to intercept her. "You're going to answer us, whether it's here or at our offices, you have to talk to us."

As he took her by the arm and tried to pull her back into the kitchen, Jen stopped. She looked down at his hand gripping her bicep and took a breath.

"Touch me again and I'll break your arm," she said. Her voice sounded a lot calmer than she felt because she could feel the anger rising inside of her like a fountain.

The agent must have realized that she meant it because he pulled his hand back. "I'm serious," he insisted. "You are going to talk to us."

"No," she answered, "I'm not. I'm going to go take my shower and get some sleep. You, on the other hand, are leaving." She stepped into the living room again and Agent Thompson made the mistake of trying to stop her again. Rather than argue the matter further, she wrenched his arm off of hers and twisted it, forcing him against a wall and curling his arm painfully high up his back. As Marc opened the door, she stepped back and shoved him through it.

"The next time you come back," she called after him, "You'd better have a hell of a lot more backup." As soon as the other three were outside as well, she slammed the door. "Assholes," she muttered in Marc's direction as she headed for the stairs.

<h1 style="text-align: center">Chapter 4</h1>

At the end of the block, a tall man stood just under the protective cover at the bus stop. He was tall, with long, wavy, strawberry blonde hair, a dark blue sweater that the saleswoman at the store where he had purchased his clothing had said brought out the color in his eyes, and a pair of basic blue jeans. He leaned against a low decorative stone wall that bordered the sidewalk and took a drink from a plastic soda bottle, slowly shaking his head. "I still don't understand it," he mused to himself. "Humans are so fascinated with this stuff and it doesn't even taste very good."

Even from where he was, he could clearly hear the sound of an interesting argument inside a house further up the street. The sounds became much more audible as the front door opened and he watched in amusement as two men quickly stepped outside into the falling snow. A third man followed the first two, and the last man to leave the house looked almost as though he had been physically thrown. The demon smiled to himself at the sound of Jen's voice as it rose in anger and he had to suppress the laughter at her threat, which he knew from experience wasn't an empty one.

"I wouldn't do that if I was you," he muttered towards the men who were leaving, even though there was no way they could hear him from as far away as he was. "She doesn't sound like she's in a very good mood."

As the four obnoxious men walked across the powder-covered lawn, he took a careful look at them. The two of them that had left the house first had power, he could sense their strength even in the human world, but the other two only acted as though they believed they had power. He smiled again as one of them rubbed the ache from a shoulder as he opened the car door to step inside. The foursome climbed into their sleek black car and drove away, not even looking at him as they passed.

Once they were gone, Thaxter turned his attention back towards Jen's house. He briefly debated on going in to see her but he knew that she wasn't alone. Normally that wouldn't have bothered him but her companions were one of the members of her response team and a werewolf, or a hybrid at the very least, neither of which did he want to become aware of his presence quite yet.

He took another drink of his soda and grimaced at the taste as he examined the label. "Why do they always have to name things so strangely?" he mused to himself as he tossed the empty bottle into a trash can. "That tasted nothing like beer."

As the bus rounded the corner and turned towards him, the demon stuck his hands into his jeans and began to walk up the street, his new shoes barely disturbing the fine blanket of snow that coated the sidewalk. As he passed in front of Jen's house, he could hear the water running upstairs and smiled to himself.

Chapter 5

When Jen headed down to the New World Response office building to report for training a few days later, her teammates were surprised to see her. J.J. was the most obvious in his surprise when he asked her, "What are you doing here already?"

"I was going crazy at the house," she explained as she opened her locker to change into workout clothes. "I need to beat on something before I go completely around the bend."

"Are you sure you're ready to get back into it already?" Marc asked. "You can take more downtime if you need it."

She shook her head and pulled her worn blue shirt over her head. "No, I'm fine. There's only so long I can stay cooped up inside the house, even if it is bigger than the old one."

Marc interrupted to pull Jen off to the side before she could hit the mat. "You haven't been to see your therapist yet, have you?" he asked as soon as they were out of earshot.

She shook her head. "I'm fine," she insisted. "I don't need to go talk to anyone about it, I just want to move on and forget it happened."

"This isn't just for you," he sighed. "We're required to provide therapy for anyone that's been in an overly-traumatic situation." He looked down and met her eyes. "You can't deny that you've been through something pretty bad."

"I know and I understand what happened. I'm not in denial about it or anything. But you're required to provide, which you've done. I'm not required to accept the offer, though."

He shook his head. "You don't understand. With the NPIB here hanging over us, you need to go see him and the sooner the better. If you don't go soon, David might not have any choice but to put you on leave until you do."

Jen blinked up at her unit leader for a long moment while his words registered. "I hadn't realized that you guys were getting flack over it like that," she finally admitted. Her eyes fell from his and she examined the toes of her shoes. "Fine," she reluctantly agreed. "I'll go see him." She looked up at Marc again and then over towards the training room. "For now, I just want to go beat on something, is that okay?"

Marc nodded and they headed over to the training room where the rest of the team was already out on the mats and working up a sweat. When Jen and Marc stepped onto the mat, however, they all stopped to look over at her. "Everything okay?" Mike asked.

"Yeah, everything's fine." She stepped closer to the three men. "Who wants the beating to-day?"

Ty smirked and stepped forward. "You really think you're going to be able to take me this time?" He bent his knees and lowered himself into his favorite stance. He gestured for her to attack. "Come get some."

She launched across the mat at him, trying to find an opening in his defense. Even as they sparred, she could tell that he was taking it easy on her. She narrowed her eyes at the realization, took a half step back, and kicked him as hard as she could in the chin. She had never hit him with a side snap kick before and it obviously surprised him.

He stood straight up and took a couple steps backwards, raising his hands in the signal to wait a moment. "What the hell was that?"

"That was you, letting your guard down," she explained as she advanced towards him.

Everyone took turns sparring against each other for the rest of the afternoon. While they trained, the conversation revolved around Animal Instincts, which was apparently a group of pro-human activists that had been picketing at City Hall over the last couple days. "I heard about them," Jen explained once J.J. filled her in on who they were, "they were on the news while I was in the hospital."

"Yeah, they seem to believe that vampire rights need to be revoked again. They've been all over town handing out fliers and telling their garbage to anyone that'll listen." He took a drink from his bottle of water and scowled. "They're using the recent vampire attacks to scare people into agreeing that all of the vampires need to be taken out."

"Yeah, but I think they picked the wrong town this time," Ty snickered. "The mayor isn't about to fall for their crap, no matter how much they want to picket about it."

"Why not?" Jen asked.

Ty looked over at her in surprise. "Because the mayor's one of our biggest supporters," he explained. "He's known for being sympathetic towards paranormals, that's why there're so many more of them here than in a lot of the other towns."

"If that's the case, then what good does this group think it'll do to protest here?" she asked. She hadn't been aware of the support from the mayor, nor had she been aware that their town had a higher quantity of paranormals than usual. Sahara was right, she realized. She really needed to do a better job of paying attention to the news.

"Because they're idiots," Mike answered. "They've been out protesting like this for probably a good six or seven months now, maybe even longer. They're just getting a lot more notoriety about it now."

In the middle of their workout, they were interrupted by a visit from David. He stepped into the training room, followed by Charlie, and whistled to get their attention. Once everyone had stopped and was looking at him, he said, "Go get geared up. There's something causing some havoc out on the highway and causing massive pileups. The police called us for backup because they can't get close enough to even see what is going on. They're in the process of blocking off the road in both directions so that there aren't any more cars getting stuck in the mess but they still don't know what is causing it."

As a group, the team jogged towards their lockers and changed into their response gear. David stopped Jen as she headed for the elevator. "Are you sure you want to do this?"

"Look, I'm fine, okay? I don't need the damn therapy but Marc told me that you'd get in trouble if I don't go, so I will. Tomorrow. But for today, I'm still capable of doing my job!" She glared at Charlie, certain that he was at least part of the problem. She knew that he was NPIB, and they were the ones putting pressure on her company and insisting she see the stupid therapist. "Now can I go?"

David stepped out of the way and let her join the group on the elevator. As the doors closed, Jen breathed a sigh of relief. For a moment, she was afraid that David and Charlie were going to make her stay behind.

They drove to the highway and from a few blocks away they could tell where the problem was. There were cars and trucks everywhere, most of them piled up on the side of the road. A couple of them had been knocked onto their sides. People, trying to escape, ran past the response trucks as they pulled into the area. Some of the vehicles that they drove past still held people, some alive but most were already dead.

Police cruisers were parked amidst the wreckage and a handful of officers worked to free the people who were still trapped inside their vehicles. Other officers directed the injured people who could still move under their own power towards a group of ambulances waiting just off the highway, out of the danger zone.

Jen ran for the closest vehicle that had movement inside, a small white sedan that was still upright but had been badly smashed in the commotion. She wrenched on the door, trying to get it open, even putting a foot on the side of the car to get some added leverage as she yanked on it. A young woman screamed and cried on the other side of the glass, pounding on the windows inside the car and Jen realized that the girl was barely even old enough to drive. With help from Ty, she ripped the door open and pulled the frightened girl free. They handed her over to the closest officer and moved further into the havoc.

Further up the road, sounds of more wreckage could be heard. The screeching of fatigued metal joined the screaming of the trapped and wounded people. The sounds echoed in Jen's head, reminding her of the screams of the victims in the demons' lair where Cylin had tortured them. Jen's howls of rage joined the screams of fear that sounded from everywhere and she ran towards the source of the commotion, ignoring the calls of her team as she went.

Whatever it took, she was going to make it stop.

Once she crested the slight hill in the highway, she could finally see the source of all of the mayhem. A young-looking man stood it the center of the highway, laughing maniacally and gesturing towards the cars that littered the road. As she watched, quickly joined by the rest of her team, the man pointed at a pole that held power lines and laughed again. The power lines stretched towards his outstretched hands, creaking under the strain until they let go of their bindings and flew towards him. The lines stopped before reaching him but even from where she was, Jen could tell that the cables were still alive with electricity.

The man swung the lines around, without ever touching them himself, and began slapping the cables against the wrecked cars that lay scattered everywhere. When he spotted an elderly man escaping from beneath an overturned van, he swung the power line his direction and sent the man scrambling back into the van. Jen's blood ran cold as she watched the man scurrying for safety, and she scanned the area, looking for a safe way to get to the people who were still trapped by the lunatic.

More bodies were scattered but the laughing man seemed unaware of them. He gleefully swung the power lines around, hitting cars, trucks, and the ground almost haphazardly. Seeing what the maniac was up to, Marc called back to David. "Can we get the power company to shut down the power out here? It looks like a psychic and he's having a blast with the power lines."

"I'll see what I can do," David called back over the radio, "but it might take a little while, so be careful."

"Great," Marc muttered as he surveyed the area. "Looks like we get to do this the hard way."

Since she hadn't been seen yet, Jen peeked around a vaguely pickup truck-shaped chunk of metal and surveyed the area again. "I think there may be a way down over there," she called over to the team. She pointed off to the side of the road where most of the vehicles had landed.

"If we stay behind those, we should be able to move closer before he realizes we're here."

J.J. nodded his agreement. "We might get some more of the people out that way, too."

They snuck closer to the amused psychic and everyone started working towards freeing the trapped people that they came across. Luckily, the man with the power lines was engrossed enough in his own entertainment that he didn't notice them until they were almost within firing range.

He held the power lines aloft and surveyed the group. When his eyes fell onto Jen, his grin slowly changed into a satisfied smirk. "So, you're still around after all," he called out to her. The power lines crackled and hissed as they released their deadly power into the air but he maintained control of them and aimed them at Jen and her team.

Jen looked over at the man in confusion, trying to figure out where she knew him from. He looked vaguely familiar but she couldn't place where she had seen him before. For that matter, she wasn't sure why he had singled her out of the group. "Do I know you?" she called over to him.

"Of course you don't," he replied. "Just like you didn't know me the last time we met." As he moved the power lines towards her, Jen realized two things. First, she was out of range of the electrical leads that he was playing with and second, she *had* seen him before. A few months ago, the same psychic had attacked her while she was in the drive-through of her favorite fast-food restaurant. Just like he was trying to do now, he had smashed cars off the road and ripped down power lines in an attempt to electrocute her.

Last time, however, she had almost been squashed by a falling pole that the lines had been attached to, so she looked around quickly to be sure that she wouldn't fall victim to the same attack again.

When the psychic had previously come after her, she hadn't known what his motivations had been but with everything else that had happened since then, she had all but forgotten about him. Now, it looked like history was about to repeat itself. She just hoped she survived it again.

"You can make this easier for everyone," he called out to her again. "Hand yourself over and I will let the rest of your team leave."

"Let me think about it," she called back, not trusting what he said. Beyond that, she was pretty certain that she didn't want to know what he would do with her if she did turn herself over to him. "No, I don't think I want to do that."

"Maybe you should consider the rest of these people," he said as he waved the power lines toward the van that still held the trapped man. "They're all just innocent bystanders. I'm sure they would appreciate your sacrifice. After all, isn't saving people what you're supposed to do?" He emphasized his threat with another arc of sparks as the power lines thrust toward the terrified civilians.

"Keep him talking," Mike whispered over to Jen as he opened his gear bag. Unlike everyone else on the team, Mike had a modular rifle, one that could be broken down into a handful of pieces so that it could fit in his travel bag.

He had gotten the upgraded rifle because he was the best distance shooter on the team and he could carry it to where it was needed, without having to deal with the bulk of a full-sized, single-piece weapon. Now, he just needed a minute or two to assemble the pieces before he could take the shot.

Jen nodded at him and turned back to the psychic. "Sacrifice?" she called over to him. "Does that mean you plan to kill me, then?"

"Of course I plan to kill you," he laughed. "Why else would I go through all this effort to get you to come to me?" He stepped closer to her hiding place, still holding the power lines in midair.

Jen looked over at Mike, who was still snapping pieces of his weapon together. "Almost done," he whispered over to her. "Just a few more seconds."

Whether the psychic had realized something was up or he had heard Mike's whisper, Jen couldn't tell. He stopped advancing and looked around as though he was trying to find something. Jen felt the familiar tug as he began swirling his energy around him. It was like a whirlpool of motionless wind, drawing more power out of everything it touched along the way. She wasn't sure what he was doing but she was positive that it wouldn't be good for her, the team, or any of the other people who were still trapped in the danger zone.

"Got it," Mike said as he slammed the extended clip of his rifle home. He raised himself to a knee and lowered the rifle across the hood of the smashed car he had taken cover behind. Barely peeking his head over the metal shield, he adjusted his angle with the rifle and fired.

The report echoed through the area, one of the loudest rifle shots that Jen had ever heard. The round tore through the maelstrom of energy that the psychic had gathered around himself, straight and true at the psychic's head. Too late, Jen realized what the psychic had been doing with the energy.

The round deflected off the psychic's energy shield, ripping into a nearby vehicle. Thankfully, the vehicle it hit was unoccupied, as the speedy bullet passed through the fiberglass as though it wasn't even there. The psychic laughed again and slammed the ground with the power cords, arcing all of the released electricity into the air and sending it flying at Mike. Licks of blue-white fire jetted past the rifleman, who stayed surprisingly calm. Blinking once and exhaling slowly, he fired another shot.

Just as before, the round deflected off the psychic's power shield. This time it landed harmlessly on the ground next to him, which the psychic appeared to find tremendously amusing.

"You really think your weapons will work against me?" he called out to them amidst his crazed laughter. "ME? You have no idea what you're dealing with!"

As he sent more lightning through the air at her team, Jen felt the world slow down. She heard her heartbeat, slow and steady, and she could smell and taste the power that the psychic was playing with. Slowly, she reached out a hand to touch it.

The power continued to swirl through the air but as she moved her hand through it, she could feel the energy begin to pull away from its psychic controller. She pulled harder, de-termined to rip the energy shield away from the insane man completely. "Hang on a second," she muttered towards Mike. "Hold your fire."

Gritting her teeth, she focused everything she had on pulling the energy from the psychic, and she could tell immediately that he knew it. His laughter faded as the power lines fell to the ground and he looked around, wide-eyed as though he was searching for the source of the interference. With another tug, she felt his hold on the energy shield release and she almost fell onto her back as the tension went slack. "Now!" she called over to Mike as she reached a hand behind her to stabilize herself against the ground.

The report sounded even as she called but she knew that it was already too late. The psychic, his energy shield gone, knew that he didn't stand a chance against a trained sniper and had used the one trick he still had available to use: cover. By the time Mike had released the first round, the psychic was already on the ground and rolling behind one of the cars that he had destroyed.

J.J. and Ty were on their feet immediately, running to where the man had disappeared behind a faded brown station wagon. By the time they arrived, however, the psychic was nowhere to be seen. They stopped and looked around, spreading out and searching for where he might be hidden but there was no sign of him.

Shaking his head, Ty looked over at the rest of the group and shook his head. "He's gone," he called out.

While the rest of the team moved forward to help the search and release the trapped people, Jen stayed where she was. A wave of nausea had spread through her and she slumped to the ground, holding her head and trying to make the dizziness subside. She groaned, wondering why she felt so awful all of a sudden. She lowered her head and felt the nausea slowly fade but the world continued to spin.

She wasn't sure how long she was there, hunched over and trying to not fall completely to the ground before she felt J.J.'s strong arms lifting her up. He began to carry her out of the area but Jen stopped him. "Hang on," she said. "I'll be okay in a minute." The nausea had already dissipated and she could feel the dizziness slowly abate. "I just need to hold still for a couple minutes."

"No," he disagreed. "What you need is a doctor."

She shook her head, then groaned and clasped her hands against her forehead. "If you take me to the hospital, they're going to know what I did."

He let her legs fall to the ground but kept a tight hold on the rest of her, making sure that he didn't drop her completely. "What *did* you do?" he asked, his eyebrows lowered in concern as he examined her.

She leaned her head against his shoulder and sighed. "I stole his energy shield," she admitted. "That's why he couldn't block against Mike's rifle anymore."

"Stole his ..." he muttered. "How could you do that?"

She shrugged against his chest. "I learned how to on the other side." She looked around at the rest of the group, who had come over to see what was going on. "Could we talk about this later?" she asked. "I'd rather not have to discuss it right now."

"Sure," J.J. agreed, his voice heavy with misgiving. With a final look around the area to be sure that the psychic was still gone, he led her out of the wreckage. He kept an arm wrapped around her until she could walk steadily on her own but even then, he stuck close by.

Marc called back to David as they walked. "Hey, we're pulling back. All of the injured are out of the area, so we'll let the cops finish the cleanup. How are you doing on getting the power cut?"

"They should have it turned off in just a couple of minutes; I just got off the phone with the power company. They agreed to cooperate completely with us and they'll leave the power down until we have the area cleared. Once everyone's out, they'll send a team in to fix the lines and get the power back up." There was a moment of silence before he asked, "What about the cause? Did you locate the source?"

"We did," Marc admitted, "but he got away. I'll tell you about it when we get back to the office."

When they got to the line of police vehicles, Marc jogged over to the officer in charge and let him know what was going on. J.J. tried to lead Jen over to one of the waiting ambulances but she refused to go. "I'm okay now," she insisted. "I'll talk to the doctor about it in my next checkup."

"When is that?" he asked.

She shrugged. "Tomorrow, I think."

Chapter 6

Although Jen wasn't normally a morning person, she felt even less like getting out of bed the next day. It was early, she was tired, and the last thing she wanted to do was spend the day with doctors and shrinks. She groaned as the alarm sounded again and rolled over to slap the snooze button. "Why did I agree to all this?" she asked herself as she sat up to stretch.

Yawning, she got dressed and padded out of her room and down the hall towards the stairs. She still wasn't used to the layout of her new house, so she kept a hand on the railing as she approached the steps. The last thing she wanted right then was to take a header from the second story. Everyone already thought she should have a lot more problems adjusting to life back home than she did and she knew that they would never believe her if she told them it was an accident.

When she got downstairs, she followed her nose towards the kitchen, where the aroma of fresh-brewed coffee waited for her. When Troy and Patrick had first come to stay with her, she had felt cramped in her own home, not used to having extra people there. However, the longer they were there, the more used to the idea she became. Now, she was glad that there was always someone home to keep the coffeepot fresh and remind her when they were about to run out of dish soap. At least she had learned, albeit the hard way, that laundry detergent was not an acceptable substitute for dish soap.

She poured herself a cup of coffee, pleased that it was still hot. A quick glance at the clock told her that her oldest brother Patrick had only left for work about forty-five minutes before, so he had to have been the one to set the pot for her. She sat at the table and sipped at her beverage, willing herself to wake up. Now, if she could only find someone to have breakfast ready for her in the mornings, her life would be perfect.

She took another sip of her coffee and dropped her head onto the table. No, she corrected herself. If morning came a few hours later in the day, *then* everything would be perfect.

She finished her coffee and poured another cup before rooting through the fridge to see if there was anything that looked good for breakfast. With a scowl, she debated on toasting a pair of frozen blueberry waffles, but she didn't really have enough time before her appointment with Dr. McAdam to enjoy them before she had to leave. Instead, she pulled one of Troy's huge travel mugs out of the cupboard. She shook some of her chocolate-flavored crispy cereal into the cup and added milk. Snapping on the lid, she headed out the door.

The drive to the hospital wasn't that far, a bit longer of a trip than it had been from her old house but not terribly so. As usual, she cranked up the tunes and gave her speakers a workout as she drove. As much as she loved driving, it just wasn't the same without a killer sound system. Because of complaints she had regularly received from her neighbors at her old house, she kept the volume below ear-splitting levels until she hit the highway. There would be plenty of time to annoy her new neighbors later, she was sure.

When she pulled into the hospital parking lot, she lowered the volume again. Not so much to stop complaints from happening but because if she left the stereo at full blast when she parked, she would forget to turn it back down when she started the truck again. Thankfully, she found a parking spot relatively easily. There weren't a lot of people at the hospital that late in the morning; it was before regular visiting hours opened and after all the morning deliveries had been made.

Since Greg McAdam was a visiting doctor and not a part of the regular staff, he didn't have an office like the other physicians did. Instead, he had a small room at the end of a hall in the secure wing. As Jen walked down the hall, she realized how much time she spent in that particular area of the hospital. When there had been a possibility of her turning into a werewolf, she had been admitted into the secure wing because it was the only area of the hospital that was locked up well enough to keep even a newly-turned Were at bay. She had returned a few times after that, for one reason or another, but this was the first time she had returned for a checkup.

She knocked twice on Dr. McAdam's door before stepping inside. The tall, sandy-haired doctor was sitting at his desk, jotting notes in a notepad. He looked up when Jen entered and smiled warmly at her. "Hey, there! I was just starting to wonder if you were going to show up." He gestured toward a chair. "Have a seat."

She walked over to a vacant chair and sat facing the doctor. "I didn't want to," she admitted, "but I guess I didn't have much of a choice."

Dr. McAdam snickered at her admission. "I can understand that; most people don't enjoy coming to the hospital." He picked up a file from his desk. "How about we get this done and over with so you can escape, shall we?" He opened the file and laid the papers across the desk. "You haven't returned to active duty yet, have you?" He looked up at her, obviously expecting a negative response, but only nodded at her silence and bowed head. "You weren't supposed to be doing that again until after this checkup, you know."

"I know," she admitted, "but I can't handle just sitting around and doing nothing."

He sighed. "Okay. Have you actually been out on assignment yet, or just actively training for now?"

"We've been doing a little training, but I have been out on a couple of assignments." She adjusted in her seat as she spoke. "Actually, I'm supposed to talk to you about that anyway."

"Okay," he leaned back in his chair and evaluated her. "What happened?"

She explained about the psychic that had been causing havoc out on the highway and that it had been her team that was called to respond. "I was fine," she insisted as he looked at her curiously, "but as we were finishing, I started to get dizzy. I was just wondering if that had something to do with, well..." she shrugged, not even sure herself what she was asking.

He hummed for a moment as he thought. "Are you still dizzy?" he finally asked.

Jen shook her head. "No, it didn't last that long but one of my teammates all but carried me back out of the danger zone."

He asked her a lot of questions about what all had happened before taking her off to an examination room. "It sounds like it was just a case of over-exertion before you were ready for it," he explained, "but I want to check on a couple of things before saying that officially."

"Are you going to pull me off active duty?" she asked, half afraid of the answer.

"I might," he admitted, "but only if I don't like what I see here now." He looked down at her as he pulled a stethoscope out of his pocket. "I know your job is important to you and I won't pull you back unless I have to, okay?"

She winced as he lightly pressed the cold instrument to her back. He listened to her breathing and heart for a few minutes before she could feel his energy flowing into her. She gripped the edge of the table, reminding herself that he wasn't trying to hurt her, that all he was doing was getting a closer look. Finally, she couldn't take it any longer and shied away from his hands. "Could you at least warn me before you start to do that?" she asked, more than a little sheepish.

He stepped back quickly. "My apologies," he said. "I had forgotten that you could feel it when I do that. I should have said something."

"I'm just overreacting, and I know that," she conceded, "but it feels really weird right now."

He made a couple of notes in her chart. "If it makes you feel any better, I didn't find anything unusual. You seem to still be healing well and I don't see anything that gives me concern."

Jen sighed. "That's a relief. What about the dizziness?"

"I'm willing to say that you probably just pushed yourself a little too hard and a little too fast. I would suggest that you take a bit more time to ease back into your work but I doubt you'd listen." He stopped writing and looked back over at her. "Could you at least promise me to rest when you can? Take a bath, get a massage, whatever it is that gets you to relax would be a great idea. Stress has an amazingly detrimental effect on the body, you know."

She smiled at him in relief. "I'll do that as

soon as I get home." She stepped off the examination table, glad to leave.

He returned her smile. "Good to hear it and I hope you'll let me know if anything happens again, okay."

She stepped out the door. She could feel his speculative eyes on her as she left but she wasn't sure she wanted to stay there to discuss it any further right then. She wasn't entirely convinced that the dizzy spell she had experienced was due to overstressing her body and was just as convinced that Dr. McAdam believed the same. *Whatever had caused it*, she reassured herself, *was done and over with*. So long as it didn't happen again, she would be fine.

When she left the hospital, she had planned to head home before going to the office for more training but then she remembered the promise she had made to Marc. Swearing, she changed directions and went to go see her appointed therapist. She needed to stop making promises to everyone. First Marc and now Dr. McAdam. She was going to start making promises to random people on the street if she didn't knock it off soon.

Deciding that coffee was more immediately important than seeing the therapist, despite her reluctantly-given promise, she detoured to her favorite coffee shop. Beene Brothers was a fairly small chain of coffee shops, only opened recently but spreading like wildfire. Jen had been one of the first people in line on the day that the first Beene Brothers had opened, always eager to try a new coffee, and had been pleasantly surprised at how good their coffee was. She had quickly become a regular and she was fairly certain that the money she had spent on her coffee habit had funded at least one of the company's recent expansions.

Once she had her standard white mocha with a shot of coconut and somehow dodged all questions about why she had been absent for the last while, she headed down to the therapist's office, out of excuses to delay. With a sigh of resignation, she parked in the first available spot she found and walked into the office.

The therapy office was warm, almost too warm for Jen's taste. It was decorated in cream, tan, and brown and Jen couldn't help but wonder how much of the décor was to soothe the patients and how much was to hide any stains from drinks and things being dropped on the floor. She eyed her coffee, wondering, as she took a seat to wait.

Dr. Wharton was a much smaller man than Jen had expected him to be. He was dressed in polished black loafers, dark grey slacks, a white button-down shirt and a tan tweed jacket with darker colored elbow patches. Silver-framed glasses were perched towards the tip of his rather sharply-pointed nose and Jen immediately thought he looked like a well-dressed ferret. He sat at his desk, writing in a thick yellow notebook while Jen waited and she sipped at her coffee, quickly growing impatient.

After sitting there in silence for almost twenty minutes, Jen finally broke the silence. "If this is a bad time, I can come back later."

"Not at all," he said without looking up from his notes. "I will be with you momentarily." While Jen seethed, he scratched a few more notes before turning the page of his notebook and looking up at her. "You must be Jennifer Rice."

"Jen, actually. Not Jennifer."

Dr. Wharton nodded and made a note in his pad, barely glancing away from her as he wrote. "And I understand you've had a rather bad experience lately that we need to discuss, is that correct?"

Jen wasn't sure how to answer the man. Somehow, it just didn't seem right to come out and say that she had been captured and abused by a pair of demons for the last month. "I, ah…" she faltered before getting very far, so she took another drink of her coffee, wishing that it held something a little stronger than just a few shots of espresso.

Dr. Wharton pushed his glasses up higher onto his nose and peered at her. "I understand that you have been through a traumatic event, so just take your time and relax. Anything you tell me will remain in this room and this room alone."

Something about his tone irritated Jen and she tried to tell herself that she was just being overly critical because she wasn't happy about being there in the first place but she couldn't help but feel as though the doctor was patronizing her. What he had said was virtually the same thing that Dr. McAdam had told her soon after she woke in the hospital but he had never seemed to be talking down to her. Stifling her scowl with another drink of her coffee, she took a deep breath and started again.

"I was in a pretty bad situation," she told him once she felt that she had herself under control once more. "I was assaulted pretty badly and I'm not very happy about that." She looked up from her cup to meet the annoying doctor's eyes before continuing. "But I'm here now, I've healed from my injuries and the person responsible for what happened to me is dead."

Not quite true, she admitted to herself. Cylin had been the one torturing her, admittedly, along with most of the rest of the captives but he hadn't been the one to take her there in the first place. The other demon, Thaxter, had managed to escape, but for some reason that thought didn't hold any fear for her. Although Thaxter had brought her to the demon's plane to begin with, he hadn't really had any contact with her once she was there. All of the pain, all of the abuse, everything had been Cylin alone.

Perhaps that was why she wasn't afraid of the surviving demon, she supposed.

"That's a rather positive attitude to have," Dr. Wharton said as he jotted more notes. "What makes you believe that the person responsible is dead?"

She blinked at him in surprise. "Because I saw it happen," she explained. "My team came to rescue me and one of them ripped his throat out."

"I understand you were heavily medicated while you were held there," he said almost as though he hadn't been listening. "Are you sure you saw what you think you did?"

Jen heard the thin cardboard cup crumple in her hand as her fists started to clench. "Are you asking me if I imagined what happened?" she asked, incredulous. Droplets of steaming caffeine splashed onto her fingers.

"Not at all," he answered. "I was just commenting on the fact that you were unconscious when you were brought home. Have you considered the idea of hallucinations?"

"Are you serious?" she asked, not sure what the idiot was getting to. She knew that she hadn't been imagining things and, even if there had been a point where she had been halluci-nating, she knew what had happened to her, both while she was captive and when she had been rescued.

"There are plenty of drugs, drugs for which you were not screened at the hospital – and I must wonder why, precisely, just such a screen-ing did not occur - which can cause halluci-nations and other effects with long-term use. They can also have other side effects, which are actually the most common reason for the drugs to be used recreationally. Since there isn't any report of your capture and imprisonment, I have to wonder exactly what happened to you while you were..." he flipped the page in his notebook and continued, "absent." His glasses had slipped from where he had pushed them and rested once more on the tip of his nose. Jen wanted nothing more at that moment than to punch them back into position for him.

She took another deep breath and a sip of her coffee from the now-mangled cup. "I don't think this is a good idea," she said before the so-called therapist could continue his line of accusatory statements that he seemed to believe were acceptable. "Sorry for wasting your time." She stood up and turned towards the door.

"Is your job so unimportant to you that you would give it up like this?" His voice called after her. "As I understand, you are required to have five sessions before being cleared and I'm not sure I would even be willing to concede this as a real session."

Jen stopped, her hand on the doorknob. She wasn't sure how much trouble she was about to get into but there was no way she could stay here and talk to him about anything, let alone about something as personal as why she was there. At least, she recognized, if she wanted to continue not being jailed for assault. "You can report whatever you want," she said without turning back to face him, "but don't expect to see me back here again." She opened the door and stepped through it. "Ever."

Still fuming, she walked to her Jeep, slamming the last of her coffee and dropping the mangled cup onto the passenger floorboard as she fired the engine. "Asshole," she snarled as her tires caught traction and she launched out onto the road. The raw power of her heavily augmented motor soothed her, allowed her to release some of the aggression and frustration that the doctor had brought forth. Before she turned the aggression onto other drivers on the street, she considered where she should go. Much as she enjoyed driving, she needed some sort of a destination, otherwise it was nothing more than a waste of fuel.

Far too irritated to go home and relax, too angry even to head to the office and let Marc and David know what had happened, Jen headed for her only remaining place of refuge: Taco King. As she waited in line at the drive-through, she debated over whether Dr. Wharton had actually been implying what she had thought he was, or if she had just been overreacting.

As she thought about the conversation, re-playing it almost word-for-preposterous word in her mind, she decided that she hadn't been wrong. He was just a jerk. And a terrible excuse for a therapist. She felt badly for anyone who went to see him and actually bought into any of his garbage.

She ordered more than twice as much food as she normally would have for just herself, deciding that it wouldn't hurt to stop in and bring Sahara some lunch. Steaming bags of deliciousness safely buckled onto her passenger seat, she turned south to go see her friend.

Sugar and Spice was quiet when Jen arrived, as it usually was. Just past the busy downtown shopping area, it was beyond the main foot traffic that a lot of businesses aim for. The bronze urns that sat on either side of the front door, usually stuffed with brightly colored flowers, were filled with small, decorated Yule trees. White lights twinkled among the branches and brightly-colored balls hung from every available limb. As Jen walked between the urns and through the front door of the shop, the small bell attached to the top of the door cheerfully announced her arrival.

Sahara sat at one of the sprawling tables scattered across the showroom floor and her toes tapped on the soft carpet beneath her feet in time with the gentle music that wafted through the room. When the door opened, she looked up and smiled at her friend. "I was wondering how long it was going to take for you to drop in." She reached out with a foot and shoved a chair towards Jen.

Jen stepped over to the table and set the bag of tacos next to the stack of labels that Sahara was working with. Groaning, she sank into the offered seat. "What are you doing?"

"I just got more herbs in, so I'm relabeling some of the jars so I can tell which ones came from which farm," Sahara explained as she poked her nose into the bag and withdrew a pair of paper-wrapped tacos.

"Does it matter?" Jen asked as she pulled out some tacos for herself.

Sahara took a bite. "Technically, they're the same herbs but different farms have different growing systems and that can slightly change some of the properties of the herbs."

Jen wasn't sure how changing the fertilizer in a flowerbed could change that much but Sahara was one of the most in-demand herbalists in town and was quickly growing a wider, internet-based client list. If for no other reason than that, Jen had to accept that there was a difference, even if she couldn't tell what it was.

"So what's on your mind?" Sahara asked, pointedly eyeing the small creases that were prominently displayed on Jen's forehead. "Those only appear when you're angry, so what did those idiots do this time?"

Jen shook her head. "Troy and Patrick are actually behaving pretty well. I had a couple of appointments today, so I haven't been home much."

"What's going on?"

Jen explained about her checkup at the hospital and Sahara was visibly relieved to hear that the dizziness hadn't been a symptom of something more severe than it had been. Seeing that, Jen decided against worrying her friend by explaining her suspicions about the doctor's findings. When Jen told her about her meeting with Dr. Wharton, however, Sahara's expression of concern deepened to an anger all her own. "He really said that?"

"I think he was trying to imply that I intentionally dosed myself with some sort of drug, or some combination of them, and then went off to an orgy, or some crap like that, and then just hallucinated the whole thing from there."

"What an ass!" Sahara exclaimed. "You weren't hallucinating anything and we all know it!"

"I know I wasn't," Jen agreed, "but I'm not going back to see him anymore and I told him as much."

"Is that going to get you in trouble at work? I thought you had to go see that guy for you to be released back to full duty?"

Jen shrugged. "I hope I can talk David into letting me see someone else if they're going to insist that I see a shrink. Otherwise, I'll just have to figure something else out." That was definitely a conversation she wasn't looking forward to. Despite the brave face she put on for her friend, she didn't know what would happen if David decided she was a liability to the team and cut her from the company.

Sahara sighed and shook her head, handing Jen a large glass jar and a blank label. "This is Cat's Claw."

Jen stayed there for almost two hours, helping Sahara finish with the labels and plowing through the bag of tacos. Sahara made some of her famous, almost literally, relaxation tea to help Jen calm down and Jen had to admit that she had needed that. "Dr. McAdam says I need to rest more and relax whenever I am able to," she admitted.

"I know exactly what you need." Her eyes twinkled as she spoke.

Jen perked up. Anytime Sahara suggested something that was "exactly what you need," it was guaranteed to either be a lot of fun, land one or more of them in jail, or perhaps all of the above. With the mood she was in, any of that would have been fine.

"You need a girls' night out," Sahara explained. "Why don't we head to Crash this weekend?" Crash was a combination dance club and bar that had only been open for less than a year but was already the most popular hotspot in town. It was built on a large, renovated barge that floated at the marina and there were always so many people waiting to get inside that you had to arrive early to have any hope of getting in.

Jen had been there once before and had a blast, so she eagerly accepted the offer. "Who else are we going to have come with us?"

"I was thinking maybe Angie, depending on how much of a headache Eric's been giving her." Angie was another of their friends, one who had recently moved, quite accidentally, into a haunted house. The poltergeist that lived there, Eric, had initially tried to scare her off but Angie had refused to go, partly because she had nowhere else to go and partly because she simply didn't want to give in to the obnoxious spirit.

The pair hung out at the shop, discussing that weekend's plans and arranging the freshly labeled jars on the numerous shelves that lined the walls of the store. When closing time arrived, Jen helped Sahara shut everything down and lock the valuables into their secure cases. "Want to come by for dinner tonight?" Sahara offered. "I'm just planning on corn dogs but you're more than welcome."

"No, thanks," Jen declined. "Mary had to go back to school a couple days ago, Jaime left yesterday, and Todd will have to go back to work soon too, so I want to spend a little more time with him while he's still here." Mary and Jaime were Jen's sisters and Jen already missed them. She wondered for a moment if their absence was contributing to her mood but soon decided that she didn't care. After everything she had been through, she was allowed to be grumpy every now and again.

"Patrick's still sticking around, though, isn't he?" Patrick was Jen's oldest brother and he had been staying with Jen while managing a build for the contracting company he worked for.

"Yeah, he's still got some time before the place'll be finished."

"So why have you been here instead of home with Todd?"

"He's telecommuting for right now," Jen explained. "Since his office is on a different time schedule, he should be off work in about a half hour."

When Jen got back to her house, not only were Troy, Patrick, and Todd's vehicles all there but there was another black sedan that Jen didn't recognize parked in her driveway. Remembering the men from the NPIB who had been to see her the other day, her mood fell as she walked into the house. She had been dealing with more than enough jerks for one day and was entirely disinterested in dealing with another one in her own home.

As she stepped into the living room, she discovered that everyone except Todd was assembled there, apparently waiting for her. Patrick and Troy were in their respective corners, taking care to keep a decent distance between them. Dr. McAdam was there as well and so was David's NPIB friend, Charlie.

As soon as Jen recognized them, she stopped and took a step backwards, for all intents and purposes planning to make a run for the door. She wasn't sure why they were there but she knew that it couldn't be anything good. Before she was able to escape, however, Patrick took her by the arm.

"It's okay," he reassured her. "Everything's fine." He guided her back into the living room and led her over to an open space on the couch. "I know you remember Greg," he said, pointing at her doctor, "and this is Charlie. I'm not sure if you remember him or not but he's been helping us out for a while." Patrick looked down at Jen as he took a seat next to her. "He was helping us try to get you back while you were missing."

"I know, David said so, too." Jen looked suspiciously between the men, aware that there would be no escape. "What's going on?" She knew that the NPIB still had a lot of questions about her, which explained why Charlie was there, but Dr. McAdam's presence was a mystery. She had a clean bill of health, signed by him, so she wondered if one of her test results had come back with something wrong.

When she asked, however, Dr. McAdam reassured her that none of these was the case. "All of your tests have been coming back negative. What I want to talk to you about is what happened with the vampire in the hospital."

Jen looked between Dr. McAdam and Charlie, then finally over to Troy and her brother. Patrick squeezed her hand and nodded, so she sighed. "Just give me a minute; I need a cup of coffee first."

Once she was ready, Charlie started to ask her questions. Jen still wasn't sure how much to tell him, mostly because she still wasn't sure if she was going to get in trouble over her feeble attempt to help the vampire in the hospital. "I was just trying to help," she finally admitted. "A lot of people were talking about how the Vamps were being tainted by the dark energy and I thought that drawing some of it out would help him get back under control."

"I can see how that makes sense. But that vampire wasn't affected by darkness tainting. He had some sort of a drug overdose but we're not exactly sure what it was yet." He smiled at her reassuringly. "I can't say much more than that because of patient confidentiality but I can understand your logic about why you did what you did."

Jen nodded, slightly relieved. She wasn't sure how she felt about having everyone know what she had done but there wasn't really any point in hiding it anymore.

"I am curious," he continued, interrupting her thoughts. "Your chart has you listed as not possessing any magical or psychic abilities. I'm wondering what you used to draw the energy.

"Since I am psychic myself, as I know you understand, I could tell it was similar to a psychic ability but it really seemed more like someone was trying to mimic a psychic than use their own natural abilities."

Jen thought about it for a moment before shrugging. "I don't have any abilities. I was tested once as a teenager and again a couple days ago and both times I came up blank."

"Then how were you able to do that? It takes at least a minimal amount of ability to move the flow of energy, let alone to redirect where it goes."

Jen shrugged again, still not sure how to answer. "I learned it from a psychic, maybe that's why it seemed that way. But I really was tested, and I have nothing."

As she spoke, Charlie seemed to perk up. He had been silent for most of the conversation, letting Jen and Dr. McAdam talk as they had a few times before. Now, however, he interrupted their discussion. "Was it Steve?"

Surprised at his question, Jen had to blink a few times before answering. "I don't know who Steve is," she said slowly. The only Steve she knew of had been her manager at a previous job, so that couldn't be the Steve to whom he was referring.

"He's a dreamwalker that was helping us while we were looking for you," Charlie supplied. "I understood him to be a friend of yours, but I could have been wrong."

Suddenly, Jen decided that she didn't want to talk anymore. Though she hadn't ever learned his name, she recognized precisely who Charlie was asking about. Worse, he was absolutely correct. Steve, the dreamwalker she had helped some time before her capture, had visited her on a few occasions while she was in captivity, helping her to maintain her sanity and teaching her a lot about energy and how it can be manipulated.

She turned to her brother for support, but he seemed to want her to continue. She, on the other hand, didn't want to get her friend into any more trouble than it appeared he was already in. Not being either a mage or a psychic herself, she wasn't sure about the legalities of passing a skill on to another person.

Charlie correctly interpreted her hesitation and spoke up again to reassure her. "If you're worried about getting Steve into trouble, you don't have to be concerned. Not only were his actions legal and warranted, given the situation, he already told David that he had spoken with you while you were being held in Derathim."

When Patrick nodded, Jen calmed down a bit again and nodded herself, looking down into her coffee cup. "I wasn't lying," she explained quietly. "I just never knew his name." When she looked up again, she met Dr. McAdam's eyes. "That was also why I was so worried about being dizzy when we talked earlier."

"Because you were taking energy again?"

Jen explained about drawing the energy shield away from the psychic and the resulting drain it had caused in her. "It got to where I couldn't stand up anymore and J.J. all but carried me back out of there. It always made me dizzy when I did that in Derathim, but I never felt that close to passing out from it before."

"I think I understand what's going on. What are you doing with the energy once you've drawn it?"

Unsure of how to answer, Jen shrugged. "I don't really do anything with it."

"That's at least a part of your problem," he explained. "You can't just draw that much energy in and not do anything with it. Not good for you is an understatement." He explained that the first thing she needed to learn was how to dissipate the energy once she's taken it into herself. "It's an important factor in energy transferal and it takes a bit of control to be able to release a lot of energy without a catastrophic reaction."

"Catastrophic reaction?" she looked up at him in surprise. Immediately, her mind flashed back to the explosion that had gone off in the demons' lair just before her team had arrived. A part of her knew that she had been responsible for the explosion but she hadn't thought about the effects of what had happened until now. "You mean that could happen again?" She muttered, more to herself than anyone else. "Crap."

"I see." he stood up and walked to where she sat. He held out a hand towards her. "Come on, this isn't the place for me to show you."

Jen blinked at him in surprise for a moment before taking his hand. "Show me what?" She asked. "Where are we going?"

"Outside." He led her out the front door and around to the backyard of the house. "There shouldn't be too many people who can see you from here," he explained. "If you've already overloaded on energy before, it just makes it that much easier for you to overload again." He looked down at her as they walked. "That makes it even more important that you learn how to dissipate."

When he stopped, they were almost completely hidden by the house. He let go of her hand and turned to face her. Despite the chill in the air and the inch and a half of recently-fallen snow that remained on the ground, he showed no signs of feeling the cold. In fact, he hadn't even bothered to pick up his overcoat on the way out. Jen stood silently, watching him and waiting to see what he would do.

They spent over an hour while Dr. McAdam showed her how to let the energy flow through her body and out into the ground at her feet. He showed her how she could drain her excess stores of energy into anything she touched, including trees and other stationary objects besides just the ground. "This works for buildings, too," he explained, "so if you're inside somewhere and you need to release the energy, you can let it go into anything around you."

When he felt secure in Jen's ability to release her stored energy, he brought her back inside. "Later, we can teach you how to store the energy safely but I don't think that's really necessary for right now. Ideally, you would just leave the energy flow alone but somehow I doubt you can do that." He smiled down at her as he spoke, reassuring her that he was teasing.

"I really do appreciate this," she started to say, but he interrupted her.

"Don't worry about it," he reassured her. "You needed someone to teach you and I'm available." He smiled at her again. "Besides, it's for the greater good. Can't have you drawing too much energy and then having it collapse where people can get hurt, now can we?"

She sobered at the thought. "That's true." Again her mind returned to the explosion she had caused, thankful that nobody had been seriously injured in the blast. As they headed back into the house, she stopped and turned back to face him. "Can I ask you a question before you go?"

"Sure," he agreed.

"What happened to the vampire?"

"He's stable but we're still trying to figure out what went wrong with him. He's still in the hospital, mostly for his own and his family's safety. Nobody wants to run the risk of having him lose control again."

Jen opened the door. "That's good. I was worried for a while that he might have been put down."

He shook his head. "He didn't kill anyone; he didn't even really hurt anyone. As far as we can tell, he did everything in his power to make sure that the people around him would be safe. There was no reason to put him down."

Dr. McAdam and Charlie stayed for a little while longer, talking and drinking coffee, before taking their leave. Jen was a lot more comfortable with having the pair of them there after her conversation with the doctor but she still wasn't sure about how much she could trust Charlie.

Finally, she admitted to herself that she didn't have much of a choice. If he had really been there while the team was trying to get her back and had been helping them in their attempts to retrieve her, then he already knew most of what had happened to her, if not everything.

Chapter 7

Jen still felt a little jittery a few days later, not sure whether it was because of the tremendous quantities of coffee she had been drinking since her return after a lengthy stretch of time having none, or if it was just her own anxiousness to have everything back to normal in her life. Realistically, she knew that her life would never be the same as it had been before she had been taken by the demons, far too much had happened to allow for that but she was determined to adapt and continue on.

She had told David about her refusal to speak with the therapist that had been assigned to her and, after hearing how their initial meeting had gone, he had reassured her that she wouldn't be in any trouble for that refusal. He did caution her that he would be looking for another therapist for her because the need for it was still present and she would eventually have to speak with someone. Not that Jen liked the idea but she knew that there wasn't much use in arguing with him. Not as long as she wanted to stay on active duty, at least.

The time was also drawing nearer to when Todd would have to go back home. Jen was looking forward to that even less than her next meeting with a shrink. Having her brother with her again, even if it was only for a little while, had been far more comforting to her than she would have expected and she knew that there would be an enormous void in her life again once he was gone. She tried her best not to show it, however, not wanting to spoil the last few days that she had with him. The night before his flight was scheduled to leave, the pair of them sat in her room, talking like they hadn't done since they were children.

"I'm still worried about you," he told her after they had been there for a while. "I've looked you over for darkness tainting more times than I can count. There isn't much there, barely even a touch of it and I doubt it's enough for any sort of negative ramifications.

"Patrick will still be here, which helps, but I'm still worried about what'll happen to you."

"I'll be fine," she told him. "And Patrick, if nobody else, will let you know if anything happens to me."

"I already talked to him," Todd admitted. "He's going to be giving me updates for the next while, just so I can feel a bit better about not being here."

The next morning, she and Patrick took Todd to the airport. After Todd boarded the plane, they waited in the terminal until it had taken off and was out of sight before Patrick took her by the arm and gently led her back out to the parking garage. Jen felt numb, as she had known she would. The ache of missing her twin brother, the other half of herself, had started almost immediately. Thankfully, Patrick understood and didn't try to engage her in any inane small talk while he drove her home.

Patrick did insist that she needed to eat and stopped at Taco King on the way, hoping that some of her favorite foods would cheer her up a little bit. The burritos helped but even the grandest of all burritos were no replacement for Todd. Jen still felt as though a piece of her very soul had boarded the plane and flown away.

When they got back home, Jen didn't feel like sitting around and doing nothing. She puttered around the house for a bit, picking up some of the dirty dishes that had been left in the living room and dropping them into the dishwasher before running a load of laundry. While the machines worked their magic, she called over to Joel.

Joel Peters was Sahara's husband, Troy's best friend, and a close friend of Jen's as well. More importantly at that moment, he was an employee of North Bank Hospital and Jen hoped that he would have good news for her.

He was happy to hear from her but less pleased when he discovered why she was calling. "Come on, you know I can't just give out that information."

"But it's me," Jen protested. "You can tell me, I'm sure."

On the other end of the phone, she could hear her friend sigh. "I'm especially not supposed to talk about this with you. But yes, they've all been released."

Jen let out a sigh of relief. "So they're all okay now?"

"Looks like it. Bailey was the most damaged, but he was released yesterday. He was taken over to the group home last night. I don't know who's scheduled to take care of their follow-up treatment."

"That's okay," Jen said. "I just wanted to know that they're all okay." She thought about it for a moment. "I don't suppose you know where this place is, do you?"

"Not a chance," Joel snickered. "Besides, even if I did know, it wouldn't do you any good. They're still under protection, so nobody gets close to them without clearance."

Jen made a mental note to ask either David or Charlie the next time she saw either of them. She hadn't seen any of her fellow captives since her rescue and she wanted to see for herself how they were doing and ensure that they were being properly taken care of.

Having made the decision to ask, she was about to head out to the office when she saw a black sedan with tinted windows parking in front of her house. Swearing under her breath, she let Joel know that she would have to talk to him later. "Someone let the animals out of the zoo and dressed them in suits. They're about to knock on my door, so I've got to go."

"Give 'em hell," Joel laughed as he hung up the phone.

As she closed her phone, Jen swung the front door open, almost knocking one of the NPIB agents to the ground in the process. At least this time they left their pet mage and psychic home. "Now what do you want?" Despite her bravado, she wasn't sure that she could escape them another time. Granted, Patrick was still there but the agents hadn't wasted any time before coming to harass her now that Todd had left.

Agent Thompson recovered quickly, putting a hand on her doorsill to regain his balance. "We still need to talk to you," he explained. "Either you can talk with us now, or we can take you to the office to talk with you."

The other agent, Brooks if Jen remembered correctly, held up a hand to stop Agent

Thompson before he continued to speak. "We believe that there may be further tests necessary to prove both your lack of darkness tainting and any magical or psychic skill you may have."

"Didn't you guys check for that the last time you were here?" she asked as she leaned against the door jamb. Although Marc had invited them into the house last time they had been by, Jen wasn't feeling nearly as generous. "As I remember, your people found nothing."

Agent Brooks nodded. "True but it has been brought to our attention that a high enough power level can cause power to not show up on a standard test. Therefore, we want to test you with a more highly-powered mage and psychic."

"So where are they?" Jen asked, pointedly looking behind them at the men they hadn't brought with them.

"Back at the office," Brooks explained, "which is why we need you to come with us."

Jen shook her head. "You don't really expect that to work, do you?" It took a lot more effort than she would have expected to keep from bursting out in laughter at their arrogance.

Normally she wouldn't have bothered to restrain herself but she felt it was better not to antagonize them more than she already was.

"Look," Thompson interrupted his partner, "we know you're hiding something. Either you're doing it deliberately, or your brother's been covering for you. But with him gone, we need some answers."

"What exactly do you think I'm hiding?" she asked. "I willingly submitted to every test that has been put in front of me, from the first time I was checked for abilities as a child to the last time you were here to the tests my doctor ran on me three days ago. I'm not hiding anything and, to be honest, I'm starting to get annoyed with your continued insistence that I am."

"Speaking of your doctor," Thompson held out a pair of stapled papers. "We need your signature on these."

Jen took the papers, suspicious. "What are they?" she asked as she looked down at the pages.

"Release forms," Brooks provided. "All they do is let us to talk to your doctors and have a look at your medical records."

This time, Jen couldn't contain the snort of derision. "And you expect me to just sign them?" She crumpled the forms and dropped them onto the porch. "Get a warrant, if you can. I'm not even close to being that dumb."

"Afraid we'll find out about the drugs?" Agent Thompson smirked at her. When she looked over at him in surprise, his grin widened. "We spoke with Dr. Wharton."

As her eyes narrowed, his grin faded. "Are you still so sure you don't want to talk to us?"

"Get off my porch," she said calmly. "Get off my porch, get out of my yard, and get the hell away from me. The next time I see you two, I'll call it in myself for harassment."

Agent Brooks obligingly stepped backward off the porch, but Thompson had one more card to play. "Unless you willingly take yourself in for magical and psychic evaluations, we will be back with that court order we promised."

"You don't have anything to get an order on," she said, trying to sound a lot braver than she felt.

Thompson grinned one more time as Brooks physically tugged him away from her. "We have enough to be suspicious and that's plenty enough for the judge we're talking to. So I'd think really hard about what you want to do now, because if you don't comply and get yourself registered when they find something, you're going to be facing some serious jail time."

Without a word, she shut the door.

Chapter 8

Only a couple of hours after the agents left, when Jen had finally settled down and was no longer raging about their threats, she noticed a sleek black car pulling up in front of her house again. When the doorbell rang, she answered it, eager to light into the agents again. "What the hell do you think you're..."

Her voice trailed off as she realized who was standing on her porch. A striking woman with perfectly coiffed dark hair, dressed in an ankle-length overcoat and impossibly high heeled boots stood there, with a man in a business suit and hair that was slightly graying at the temples at her side.

"Mom? Dad? What are you doing here?"

"Is that any way to greet your parents?" Janice

Rice asked as she breezed past her daughter and into the house. "Seriously, Jen, people are going to start to believe we raised you without any manners whatsoever."

Jen stepped back to let her father, Dean, into the house as well. Unlike his wife, Dean stopped to hug her before stepping into the entryway. "It's good to see you, sweetheart," he said as he wrapped her in a tight embrace.

"At least it looks like you've been doing well for yourself," Janice commented as she looked around the living room. At her appraisal, Jen was glad that she had been making some effort to keep at least the front half of the room from looking like a tornado had passed through it. Her eyes roved around the spacious room, barely even touching down on the plain furnishings before turning to meet Jen's. "Yule is almost here, why haven't you decorated?"

Jen sighed and closed her eyes, stifling an oath. Among all of the other things that had been going on, she had completely forgotten that this was her year to host the family Yule gathering. "I've been pretty busy lately," she started to explain but her mother interrupted her yet again.

"Todd mentioned that this wasn't a good time for you, so that's why we decided to come early and help you get ready." She looked back into the living room and then over to the staircase that led up to the bedrooms. "Although I think we're going to need to get a few more decorations. This place is quite a bit larger than your last place was."

She looked back at Jen without missing a beat. "Tradition is tradition after all. I don't understand all of what is going on with you lately but I'm sure it isn't anything that would interfere too much with this year's holidays."

"Actually..." Jen started to explain once more but this time she was interrupted by the front door opening behind her.

"Hey, did those guys come back again?" Troy's voice called out as he stepped into the house. "I thought they weren't going to without a court order." His voice trailed off as well as he stepped into the living room. He looked from Jen to her mother and then to her father before returning to Jen again.

"Troy, this is Janice and Dean, my parents," Jen introduced him.

Dean nodded politely, evaluating the hybrid visually without saying anything but Janice turned immediately to gush at him. "My goodness, it's a pleasure to meet you! An absolute pleasure." She stepped towards Troy and took him by the hand, pulling him further into the room. Troy turned pleading eyes towards Jen, but there was nothing she could do.

"Todd had mentioned you, of course, but we hadn't heard very much from Jen," Janice continued to pull Troy into the living room, guiding him over to the couch and bidding him to sit next to her so that they could talk more. "Now, I want to know much more," she said, looking between Jen and Troy. "For example, how long have the two of you been together?"

Troy visibly choked at that point, his eyes widening and looking questioningly at Jen once more. He tried to stammer a response, but it was useless under Janice's interrogating smile.

"Mom, it's not like that," Jen decided that it was best to interrupt before her mother went too far overboard. "He's not my boyfriend, he's my roommate."

Janice looked up from the hybrid to meet her daughter's eyes. "Yes, I'm sure of that, which explains how you're able to live in such a nice house on your salary." She turned back to Troy and continued her barrage. "But I can tell when there's more going on, so don't you think you can fool *me*." She giggled, a high-pitched noise that Jen had always thought was more appropriate for an anime schoolgirl than a fully-grown woman.

"Seriously, there's nothing going on," Patrick's voice called out from the kitchen as he walked out with a tray that was loaded down with cups of coffee. He stepped into the room and offered Jen a cup, which she accepted gratefully, before passing drinks out to his parents and Troy. "Furball here's a friend of Sahara and Joel's and Jen's been letting him stay with her as a favor to them."

"Is that so," Janice sniffed as she took a sip of her drink. "Too bad," she said as she looked at the hybrid again and then over to her daughter, lowering her voice conspiratorially. "He's pretty cute."

Jen sighed in exasperation. Janice Rice wouldn't be happy until all of her daughters were settled down and married and she made no attempt to hide that fact from her children. Jen had grown up with her mother hounding her because she never seemed to have any romantic interests, unlike her sisters. For a little while, Jen had even been questioned about her sexual orientation, because her mother was determined that there had to be a reason that Jen hadn't appeared to be interested in dating. That particular line of questioning had backfired quite spectacularly the first time Mary brought home a girlfriend but it hadn't fazed Janice's insistence that all of her daughters needed to be in stable relationships, preferably resulting in marriage.

What her mother hadn't realized was that Jen had been afraid to date anyone because she knew that her mother would react exactly as she was now. She had seen it scare off plenty of boys that Jaime had brought home, and even a few girls that Mary had been brave enough to expose to Janice's examinations but Jen had decided that she would rather be single than to ever go through that much embarrassment voluntarily.

Disappointed but finally satisfied that there was nothing going on with Troy, Janice turned to face her daughter more fully. Jen sighed and took another drink of her coffee, knowing full well what was about to happen. She had lived through plenty of these discussions but at least there wasn't anyone there except for Patrick and Troy and she could handle that in front of them.

She was just glad that her teammates weren't there; they would never let her live it down.

"So who are you dating now?" She asked Jen, a clear look of expectation on her face.

Jen just shook her head and took another drink of her coffee. "I'm not," she answered. "I've been a little too busy to be out trolling for dates."

Janice sighed. "Why do you have to put it so crudely?" She took another sip of her own drink and shook her head. "You're not get-ting any younger, you know. If you don't start looking soon, you aren't going to have very many options left when you decide you don't want to be alone anymore."

"To be perfectly honest," Jen looked directly at her mother as she spoke, "I don't *want* anyone right now. I've had a couple of really bad experiences and I'm not that eager to jump into anything new right now." She took a drink of her coffee without breaking eye contact. "Besides, with my new job and all, I don't really have a lot of time to deal with it."

Janice scowled at her. "Yes, I had heard that you lost your job with that security company you were working at. Honestly, I don't know why you wanted to work in a place like that anyway. You need a much safer place to work, maybe a nice comfortable office position."

"I'm still in a version of security but now I work with a paranormal response agency. It's a lot better," Jen said as she drained the last of her cup. "It's a lot more challenging than sitting at the port all night and watching the ducks swim by."

"Paranormal response team?" Janice looked up in surprise. "You mean like one of those places that have been all over the news lately?" She searched for a coaster to set her cup down on the coffee table but, finding none, she pulled a napkin from her bag to rest it on before folding her hands on her lap. "That's an awful place to work, why would you want to be there? It looks like that'd be even more dangerous!"

Jen stepped towards the kitchen to refill her cup. "It is more dangerous but it pays a heck of a lot more and I like the team I'm working with." She looked over at Patrick and Troy before stepping into the kitchen. "It's nice to work with people I know I can trust."

While Jen refilled her cup and worked on calming down, she could hear her father as he tried to calm Janice down. "It's her life, after all. She's allowed to work for whoever she wants to."

By the time Jen came back out to the living room with her fresh cup of coffee, her parents were getting ready to leave. She looked over at them curiously as they headed towards the door. Seeing her gaze, her father called over to her.

"We're heading down to the hotel. We already

checked in, but I think your mother needs a little rest to recover from the jet lag."

Jen followed them over to the door. "I would let you guys stay in my old place but some of Patrick's coworkers are already moved in."

"Don't worry about it," Dean reassured her. "The hotel is nice and it has room service." He escorted his wife out the door before turning back to hug his daughter and give Patrick a firm handshake. "Take care of her, now," he said to Patrick before turning back to Janice.

"I will," Patrick pulled the door closed behind them. He turned to Jen. "Are you okay?"

"I had completely forgotten that it was my year to host." She ran a hand through her tangled hair. "Actually, I had almost forgotten that Yule was coming up." She looked around the entryway. "I don't even know where my Yule decorations are."

"I got you covered on that one," Troy spoke up. "I made sure to have them somewhere that we could get to them easily, just in case you wanted to decorate this year." He grinned at the pair of them sheepishly. "I hadn't been aware that you were going to have family coming over, or else I would have already pulled them out of storage for you."

Patrick shook his head. "I know Todd called them to let them know that nobody was going to make it out for Yule and that Jen's been over-worked a bit. I had thought that the celebration had been called off after that but apparently Mom's still as stubborn as ever."

Jen took a long drink of her coffee. "No, it's okay. We'll just get the decorations up and everything'll be fine. We just need to keep them from finding out everything that's been happening lately." She looked over at Troy. "Since you know where they are, would you mind pulling the decorations out?" When he nodded and headed for the stairs, Jen looked around the lower floor of the house.

"Mom's right," she said over to Patrick while chewing absently on her lower lip. "This place is a lot bigger than my old place was, so I probably don't have enough decorations to cover it."

"That's okay," he reassured her as he reached out to rub her arm with one large, well-calloused hand. "We can take care of that later. How about you go get another cup of coffee and calm down for a bit and I'll go help Furball get the decorations going."

Jen turned towards the kitchen again. "Thanks," she called after Patrick as he headed for the stairs to catch up with Troy. "I appreciate this."

"Hey," he grinned down at her, "what are big brothers for?"

She snickered at him as he bounded up the stairs, and the sound of the two men arguing could soon be heard floating down from above. Secure once more that everything was as it should be, Jen stepped towards the kitchen to refill her cup.

Before long, Troy and Patrick started hauling boxes of Yule decorations downstairs and gathering everything in the living room. Jen sat among the boxes and began separating the boxes into indoor and outdoor decorations. The steady lights went into the outside pile while the twinkling lights stayed inside. Before too long, she realized that she would need to make a third pile, which consisted of decorations that would work either inside or outside, depending on where they decided they would look best.

The men took the lights outside and Patrick pulled a ladder from the rack on his truck so that they could climb up to the roof and begin hanging them. While they were busy, Jen carried boxes of décor that would stay inside and began to separate it out into which rooms would be decorated with what items. She hung the strands of tiny, sparkling lights in every window that faced out the front of the house, recognizing that there weren't nearly enough to do the other three sides as well, and evaluated the boughs of Yule greenery, wondering where to put them.

When she came to the box that held all of her holiday music, she pulled out one of her favorite CDs and plugged it into her sound system and cranked it up, certain that the carols could be heard at the end of the block. With a shrug, she decided that it wasn't too loud after all and went back to work, humming along with the music as she decorated.

Before she was finished with the kitchen, however, her phone rang. Recognizing David's number, she answered it. "Hey, boss. What's up?"

Silence greeted her on the other end of the line for a moment before she could hear David chuckling. "Getting into the holiday spirit, are we?"

Jen grinned, able to hear the smile in her boss's voice. "My parents just showed up in town and they reminded me that I hadn't put anything up yet. So I put the guys to work and needed a little bit of mood music to get this done."

David's chuckle turned to all-out laughter as she explained. "That sounds like fun. But I was calling you because you had asked about the other hostages that were released with you."

Her attention caught, Jen stepped over to the stereo and turned the volume down. The visit from her parents had distracted her from going down to ask about them again personally, for which she felt chagrin. Had she just gone when she had intended, David wouldn't have needed to call her now. "Is everything okay?" she asked. "Did something happen to one of them?"

"No, they're all doing just fine. But you had been asking to go see them and I wanted to let you know that I got clearance for you to visit."

"That's awesome!" Jen exclaimed as she set down the ribbon-riddled greenery that she had been trying to untangle. "When can I go see them?"

"Whenever you want," David answered. "I have their address and your pass here whenever you want to come pick them up."

"Decorations can wait," Jen told herself as she hung up the phone. She had barely gotten any updates on how the other captives had been doing since their rescue and, although she believed that they had been taken care of, she wouldn't be happy until she saw it for herself. Beyond that, a factor that she wasn't sure she was ready to face yet, was the realization that bonds had been formed during her time in captivity and she just plain missed them.

At the office, Jen stormed into David's office. Not surprisingly, he was waiting with an envelope that had her name scrawled across it. He looked up from his watch and grinned at her as she dropped into a chair. "I think you just broke a land-speed record getting here," he teased.

She grinned back at him. "I didn't even run any red lights." Her driving talents had been the basis of many jokes since she had received her license and it didn't seem to matter where she was, someone was bound to give her grief over her heavy-footed use of the accelerator pedal and almost complete disregard of the brake.

He handed over the envelope. "You can go see them as soon as you want to, but I don't want you to be getting too excited. They're all physically healthy, Greg already saw to that, but most of them are still pretty destroyed, mentally. They have a therapist working with them as well – not the same one you saw," he added quickly at her expression, "but it hasn't been long enough to see much by way of im- provement yet."

Jen nodded soberly. "I know, I remember how they were while I was there." She looked up from the envelope to meet David's eyes. "Rationally, I know that there are a lot of people already keeping an eye on them but I need to feel like I'm doing something too."

"I can understand that," he admitted. "Go on, then." He smiled again as she stood up and headed for the door.

"I just hope this helps you, too," he said in a much more subdued voice once she was gone.

Chapter 9

The house that the group had been placed into was large, but Jen still thought it looked a bit too cramped for that many people to reside in comfortably. She parked at the curb and double-checked the address that David had given her before turning off the ignition and stepping out into the lightly-falling snow. Taking a deep breath of the chilly evening air, she stepped across the yard and up to the front porch to knock.

A woman in her late forties answered the door. She had short brown hair streaked with grey and her face was lined with years of stress. She wore a white smock with a name tag that read Maureen and blue jeans over a pair of the most uncomfortable-looking shoes Jen had ever seen. She eyed Jen suspiciously, with an expression that was just short of outright hostility.

"I'm here to see the group," Jen started to explain but Maureen interrupted her.

"Nobody's allowed to see them without authorization," she said as she started to close the door.

Jen placed her foot in the door's path and stopped it from closing as she pulled the envelope out of her pocket. "I have documentation right here." Although Jen could appreciate that it was obviously this woman's job to keep people out, there was no reason for her to be as aggressive about it as she was. However, Jen had papers that were signed not only by David but by Charlie as well so there was no reason for her to not be allowed to enter.

Maureen took her papers and examined them, a small crease on her forehead deepening as she read. She grudgingly handed them back to Jen once she was finished and opened the door to let her in out of the snow. "Just don't rile them up," she cautioned Jen as she closed the door behind her. "There's no telling what would happen if you did."

Jen looked at the woman in confusion but decided to hold her tongue. To hear the way Maureen had said it, it seemed as though the group had become violent or something. Jen wasn't sure why, but she was positive that none of them would ever try to hurt her.

She followed the woman deeper into the house and into a large meeting room. Part of the group was here, apparently in the middle of a group therapy session. Not wanting to interrupt, partly because of Maureen's warning stare but mostly because she didn't want to disturb the group's treatment, Jen took a seat on a chair behind the group to wait.

Zack was sitting in a small folding chair, his legs crossed in front of him, his arms crossed over his chest, and completely nude.

"I know this is hard for you to talk about," the therapist said as he squatted on the floor in front of him, "but we need to discuss it." He was younger than Jen's therapist had been and was dressed in blue jeans and a knitted sweater.

Zack simply glared defiantly at the man, refusing to answer him even with a nod of the head or a shrug. Jen watched in amazement as

all that hard." He smiled and shrugged towards her. "I know, still probably not the answer you were hoping for, but I hope it's better than nothing."

With another nod, Jen looked between Charlie and David. "Thank you," she said. "I know I'm being completely unreasonable, but I'm worried about them. And I don't like the situation they're in now much more than I liked the one they were in when I met them."

"I understand that," Charlie reassured her. "And I'll see what I can do to find another therapist, too. No promises on how soon I'll find one but I give you my word that I'll be looking."

Jen nodded again before stepping through the doorway, a lot more calmly than she had when she had entered. She wasn't sure how much she believed him but she knew that she had to give him a chance. Besides, she had every intention of looking for a replacement therapist on her own as well. There had to be plenty of people who were more capable of dealing with the group than Doctor Dumbass was.

As she climbed into her truck to head home, she pulled out her phone and called Sahara.

"I'm not going to be able to make it to Crash this weekend."

The disappointment was evident in Sahara's voice. "Why not?"

"Mom and Dad are in town," she explained. "Mom's already made plans for us to go out that night."

Sahara sighed. "Is she still harping on you to get married and settle down?"

"Of course," Jen grinned. "You should have seen the look on Troy's face when Mom thought he was my boyfriend."

Laughter crackled across the phone and Jen couldn't help but snicker as well. She had never seen Troy so scared and told Sahara as much.

"I believe it," she answered once she could speak again. "And don't worry about this weekend; we can reschedule it for later."

Chapter 10

The next afternoon, Jen sat on the floor of the living room in front of the coffee table to clean her pistol after her morning round of target practice. She still wasn't very good with the handgun but even she had to admit that she was getting better. After flipping on the television, she headed into the kitchen and dug through the cupboards, looking for something to snack on while she worked. Much as she hated watching the news, there were times when it was the best way to find out what was released for public knowledge and what the general population hadn't been informed of yet. Since she would be having dinner with her family that night, she figured it'd be a good idea to know what she could let them know she knew and what to keep her mouth shut about.

"Police are preparing the barricades for tomorrow's Animal Instincts rally at City Hall," the perky brunette in front of the camera said, pointing to the immense building behind her. "The rally is scheduled to start at noon tomorrow but police have already started making preparations for the expected fallout."

She pulled a half-eaten bag of ranch-flavored tortilla chips from the cupboard and wondered for a moment which of the guys they belonged to. With a shrug, she opened the bag and sat at the table again. "I can always pick them up some more later," she told herself as she popped the first chip into her mouth. Since Troy, who was parked in his recliner, didn't say anything, she assumed they were Patrick's.

When she looked back at the television, she was surprised at how much space the police were setting aside for the rally. "I hadn't expected there to be so many people," she mused as she picked up her bottle of oil and uncapped it. "Maybe they're just making sure that they have more than enough room."

She kept half an ear on the news broadcast while she worked, disappointed that she didn't hear anything really interesting. There were weather and traffic reports, a couple of feel-good stories about the local animal shelter and an expose on a new local business that had initially seemed promising, until she realized that it was just free publicity for one of the news channel's sponsors. When she was finished reassembling her pistol, she looked over at the clock and realized that she couldn't stall any more.

She tossed the remote control to Troy, who was all but foaming at the mouth in his eagerness to break in his new video game. "All yours," she said as she stood up and dropped the pistol into the lockable drawer she stored it in while she was home. "I need to go get a shower, so have fun."

By the time she hit the foot of the stairs, the hybrid had the television switched over to the gaming system and the game was already loading. She shook her head, amazed at how quickly he could move when there were mech battles to be had.

Upstairs, she turned the water on as hot as she could handle before stepping under the spray. As she let the water beat down across her shoulders and back, only stinging a little bit at the three claw marks that still decorated her shoulder, she glanced around the small, curtained area. Much as she tried to talk herself into staying calm, she couldn't help but feel exposed. The same thing had happened every time she was in the shower since being home from the hospital but she again reminded herself that she wasn't being watched, she was just being paranoid.

She reached for her shampoo, reassuring herself that there was nobody waiting outside the curtain, no angry demons or crazed psychics waiting to pounce on her as soon as she was completely defenseless. Even knowing that, she had to remind herself that she wasn't defenseless because that was why she kept a can of aerosolized pain on the shelf just outside the curtain.

The aerosol was a combination of ghost pepper oil, garlic oil, and a handful of other chemicals, all of which were designed to stop even the most determined of intruders. It had initially been designed as a vampire repellant but then it was discovered how well it worked on Weres so people started to use it as a generic paranormal repellant.

Considering the ingredients, Jen figured it'd make a pretty good psychic repellant too. In fact, there wasn't much that it wouldn't repel.

Except Troy, of course. If she didn't keep it hidden, he was likely to use it as a steak seasoning.

She finished lathering up her hair but the sense of being watched persisted. As she rinsed the shampoo out, she tried to be as silent as possible, listening intently for any sound of the intruder that she was certain was on the other side of the curtain. With the water running over her head, she couldn't hear anything but that didn't mean that there wasn't anyone there.

She knew she was being paranoid. As she did every other time the sensation overtook her, she focused on pulling in deep, slow breaths and exhaling equally slowly, a relaxation technique she had learned as a teenager. Sometimes the breathing exercises helped... but sometimes they didn't.

As soon as the water had rinsed all of the soap away, determined that there was someone there after all, Jen ripped the curtain open to grab the repellant. She shrieked as a loud noise sounded, echoing through the bathroom, and had to grab onto the towel rack to keep from falling as her feet slipped out from under her.

As her phone continued to ring, she looked around the room and realized that she was alone after all. It had just been her imagination running wild, exactly as she had known it was. With a sigh, she reached over to the counter and picked up her phone, shaking some of the water off her face as she flipped it open to answer.

"I was just calling to be sure you were going to meet us at the restaurant," Janice's voice greeted her.

"Yeah, I'm still coming," Jen answered as she carefully stepped out of the tub. She reached back to turn off the water and pulled a towel off the rack. "I'm just getting out of the shower now, so I should be right on time."

"That's good," her mother said. "You've never been very good at being on time, so I decided to give you a reminder call to be sure you hadn't forgotten."

"No, I remembered." She had a little difficulty juggling the towel and the phone but finally decided to just wrap the towel around her and let it soak up what water it could. "But I've got to go so I can get dressed, or else I *will* be late."

"Okay. We'll be getting there a bit early to get drinks before dinner, so look for us out on the patio when you get there, all right?"

"Got it," Jen answered before snapping the phone closed. She sighed as she stepped out of the bathroom and padded down the hall towards her bedroom. The last thing she wanted to do right then was to go out for a swanky dinner downtown with her parents, but she didn't have much of a choice. As she opened her closet, she sent up a silent word of thanks to her sister Jaime, the style mogul. While she had been in town, she had gone shopping for a new wardrobe for Jen, so at least she had something to wear that night that wouldn't be too out of place.

Forty-five minutes later, she parked her truck in the expansive parking lot and carefully stepped inside the restaurant. The dress that Jaime had gotten for her was comfortable enough, but the heels left something to be desired. Jen had no idea how other women could spend so much of their time balanced on a pair of toothpicks standing on end like that.

Normally, she wouldn't have been caught dead in a body-hugging dress and spike heels but if she didn't dress for the part, her mother would have a fit. With a sigh, Jen stepped into the crowded patio, thankful that at least she wouldn't know anybody there.

Her father waved at her from a table, and even Janice looked up in surprise. "Well, didn't you clean up nicely?" She ran her eyes over the black dress and heels, raising an eyebrow at the length of the hem. "Isn't that dress just a little on the short side?"

Jen looked down at her dress. Granted, the hem was above the knee, but it wasn't anywhere near as short as the ones most people were

"I just don't understand why you are so against the idea of settling down."

"I'm not ready to settle anywhere yet. Besides, Jaime hasn't gotten married either and she's older than I am."

"At least Jaime's trying. She dates, which is a concept that I'm starting to think you don't really have a grasp of." Janice took another sip of her drink and lowered her eyebrows at Jen. "Why don't you understand that you're not going to find a husband while you're out playing G.I Jane?"

"Honey," Dean interrupted as Jen fell silent, "maybe we should let it go for now. Aren't we supposed to be celebrating the holidays?"

With a sigh, Janice took another drink and regarded her husband. "I can't help it if I want to see my children settled and happy before I'm too old to enjoy my grandchildren."

"I know that," he responded, "but it's Jen's decision. Right now, she's doing something that she feels is important and she obviously enjoys what she does or else she wouldn't still be there. I think we need to be supportive of her."

To Jen's relief, the debate was cut short by

the sound of screaming on the street outside. Immediately, she popped up to see what was going on. She craned her neck to look down the block, where all of the commotion seemed to be taking place and discovered that a vampire was tearing through the crowd of shoppers. One, two, three people fell under his assault as Jen watched in horror.

"Go inside," she shouted over to her parents as she bolted for the door that led out to the parking lot, "and get down!"

She sprinted to her Jeep, wincing as she felt first one heel snap off, followed shortly by the other. She shrugged it off as she opened the rear door of her truck, thankful that she kept some extra gear stored inside in case of emergency.

As she opened the cases, she pulled out her phone and called Marc. "I've got a rampaging Vamp on the corner of fifth and Madrid," she said as she pulled out her body armor.

"Are you okay? Is anyone hurt?" he asked her.

"Yeah, he's taken out at least three people. I'm fine, just get the team moving, okay?" She set the phone down as she fought with the clasp of the armor.

"Be careful. Just monitor him until we get there," Marc's voice called up from the phone. "We just got you back; nobody wants you to get hurt right now."

"Just get the team out here. I'll be fine until then." She snapped her phone closed and dropped her armor over her shirt. More screaming reminded her that she didn't have enough time to get completely geared up, so the leather and metal shirt would just have to do for now.

She looked at her shotgun, knowing that she was better with that than any of her other weapons. "No," she told herself, "too many people." She realized that she was far more likely to hit other people as she was to hit the Vamp. Instead, she slammed a red-marked clip into her pistol, dropped a syringe of heavy-duty tranquilizer into a pocket and picked up her net launcher. In case she needed to come back for more stuff, she left the back of the truck partially open.

Back on the street, the vampire was moving quickly. He was a lot further up the street than

Jen had expected him to be and was now only a few yards from the restaurant where her parents were. Jen crossed her fingers, mentally at least, and hoped that Patrick was keeping them away from the windows. If her mother saw her like this, she'd never hear the end of it. A glance at the window let her know that her hope was in vain because she could clearly see all three of them through the big bay windows. "At least they're inside," she told herself.

Determined not to let the vampire get any closer to her family than he already was, she stepped directly into his path, praying that she wasn't making a fatal mistake. As the vampire dropped his latest victim and reached for another, Jen shouted at him. "Hey, ugly!"

He looked up and spotted her, open and apparently vulnerable, and moved forward towards her. As soon as he was in range, she lifted the net launcher to her shoulder and fired.

The net opened as it should and the Vamp howled in rage as the net surrounded him. Jen sent up a word of thanks, reminding herself that J.J. deserved at least some credit for having kept her at the range with the net launcher the business end of her pistol against the base of his skull, just in case.

When she looked up, she realized that Patrick was there as well, his own pistol pointed at the vampire. "Are you okay?" he called over to her.

Jen nodded in response. "I think I've got him for the moment," she called back over to him. "But would you go grab the black case out of the back of my truck?"

By the time she finished speaking, Patrick was up and moving. When he came back, he had her small black case in one hand and still had his pistol in his other hand, trained steadily on the Vamp.

Jen took the case and opened it. Inside, more syringes were ready and waiting in case she needed them. Next to the row of tranquilizers were a few sets of shackles, all of which were placed alongside another canister of pain, identical to the one she had in her bathroom at home. She pulled out a set of shackles and began to cuff the groggy vampire.

When the team arrived, Jen and Patrick had managed to drag the sleeping vampire out of the middle of the sidewalk and attach him to a street light pole. None of the people who had been attacked by the Vamp had survived but at least it didn't appear that any of them were going to become vampires themselves. Just to be sure, the brother-and-sister pair guided shoppers and onlookers around, not letting anybody get close to the carnage.

Marc and the team actually arrived sooner than Jen had been expecting, followed by a pair of ambulances with lights and sirens blaring. Jen waved her team over and pointed the emergency crews toward the vampire's victims. As far as she could tell, the vampire had taken out over a dozen people, including those he had killed before Jen had spotted him. She knew that there was almost no hope of saving him, but she was glad that she hadn't been forced to kill him herself.

J.J. came over to her immediately. "Are you okay?" he asked her, his eyes full of concern. "Marc said you took him down on your own."

"I was hardly alone," she corrected him. "Patrick was here too."

Jen's team didn't take very long to get the

vampire carted off and the paramedics took care of his victims, so less than half an hour after their arrival, Marc came over to see Jen. "You look like you were out on a date," he pointed out.

She shook her head. "Dinner with the family," she explained.

"Are you still going to be able to come in and file your reports?"

"Yeah, but I'll be a few minutes behind you guys." She looked over her shoulder, where she could see her parents watching intently out the window. Janice had another drink in her hand and Jen wondered how many of them she had consumed so far.

"No problem. Just get in as soon as you can, okay?" When she nodded, he clasped her on the shoulder. "Not quite what I meant by monitoring him, but you did pretty good out there."

"Thanks." As the waiter brought Janice yet another rum and cola, Jen decided that it was time to head in and face the music. "I'll be at the office soon." With a deep breath, she picked up her net launcher and the case full of syringes and headed into the restaurant.

Most of the patrons had already left during the commotion, so it was easy to find the table that Dean and Janice had been seated at. Jen walked over to the table and looked between them sheepishly. "I think I'm going to have to take a rain check on dinner," she said. "I have to head into the office and file my reports."

Janice looked at Jen, her eyes roving from her tousled hair to her worn leather armor shirt and finally down to her destroyed shoes. "I think what you need is to go home and get cleaned up." By the slurring of her speech, Jen was sure that she had more than just a couple too many drinks. Just how many rum and colas had she managed to drink while Jen had been outside?

Jen shrugged. "Technically, since I was the first one on the scene, I'm supposed to get my reports turned in immediately. I have a change of clothes in the truck, so I can get cleaned up at the office."

"You go ahead and do what you need to do," Dean stood up and hugged her. "Patrick already told us that you weren't hurt and that we shouldn't worry too much."

the edge of the street. "This Yule is gonna be great."

"Shouldn't worry?" Janice's voice rose to a shrill pitch. "She just took on a vampire single-handedly and you're still trying to tell me that I shouldn't worry?"

Jen wanted to point out that Patrick had been there as well, but she didn't want to make her mother any more irate than she already was. "How about you guys go get some rest and I'll call you tomorrow. We can get together then, or later on in the week, okay?"

Dean nodded and helped Janice to her feet, assisted by Patrick.

"I'll help them get home," Patrick informed her. "Do I need to file a report too?"

Jen shrugged. "It probably wouldn't hurt. I'll ask David when I get in and let you know." Glad for the excuse to escape but knowing that this would only make things worse later, Jen turned and headed for the door. Her truck was still parked where she had left it and she stopped to put her armor and gear box into the back of the truck before heading down to the office.

"Yep," she grumbled as she crunched through the thin layer of ice that had accumulated on for the therapist's benefit because he still wasn't wearing any clothes. He sat on one end of the couch, leaning against the armrest and idly watching the rest of the group. Bailey sat on the floor next to his feet, leaning back against the couch with his eyes closed and his head lowered. Jen thought for a moment that he might have been asleep but there was a sense that he was far more aware of what was going on around him than he was letting on. The appearance of sleep was probably a hold-over from his time spent in captivity.

Jon and Andre, a tall lanky man with bright violet hair and eyes to match, appeared to be having some sort of an argument. Andre was sitting in the only reclining chair in the room, both hands and both feet securely attached to the chair. Jon, on the other hand, had both arms wrapped around Andre's torso and was trying to bodily lift him out of the seat. All he was managing to do was lift the man and the chair, much to everyone else's amusement.

Christy, a shapely young woman with pale blonde curls cascading down her back, sat quietly in front of a small coffee table, watching the men and carefully plucking pieces of meat, crackers, and slices of cheese off of a plate that was piled high with more of the same.

Two more girls sat near her, one was a thin brunette with red highlights in her hair and bright blue eyes, and the other was a girl with skin the color of milk chocolate and short black hair. The brunette sat in silence, watching the men argue but the darker-skinned girl laughed in open amusement.

"But that's my chair!" Jon exclaimed as he tugged on Andre again. "I was sitting there first."

"You moved," Andre argued. "So you weren't here anymore."

"I moved to get a snack," Jon protested as his grip on the wiry young man slipped and he stumbled backwards. Grumbling anew, he looked down at the table, only to discover that his pile of snacks had diminished significantly.

He looked at the girls accusingly but without real malice. He pouted as he stepped forward to reclaim his plate, only then discovering that he had more of an audience than he had expected. "You're back!"

Everyone turned to see what he was looking

the small, docile Zack she had known in the demons' lair showed a bit more strength of will than she would have expected. Wisps of hair fell barely over his eyes but did nothing to hide the seething contempt that he kept contained inside.

When the therapist realized that he was getting nowhere with Zack, he moved to the young man sitting in the next chair over. Jen couldn't immediately identify who that person was, as his back was to her, but there was something familiar about the light brown hair that hung just past his shoulders. As the therapist squatted down in front of him, the man turned in his seat and pulled his feet up onto the chair in front of him, wrapping his arms protectively around his blue jean-clad knees as he moved. His olive-green shirt draped loosely from his arms, as though it had been picked for a much larger person.

"And how are you today?" The therapist asked him, leaning forward and putting his hands on either side of the young man's slender hips. "I see you've gotten dressed, that shows a bit of progress."

The young man cringed away from him again, turning even further away from the therapist. As he twisted his head to look away, Jen discovered that his eyes were clenched tightly shut, and an expression of obvious fear was clearly written across the poor man's face. With a start, Jen realized that the man she was looking at was Bailey, and her heart broke to see him in such obvious distress. She had known that he wasn't doing well, as she understood he had been the last to be released from the hospital but she hadn't expected to see him like this.

As the therapist continued to prod at Bailey, encouraging him to respond, Bailey continued to flinch away from him. When the therapist leaned closer to encourage eye contact, there was an audible whimper as tears began to flow down Bailey's face. As Bailey tried to turn his face further away from the therapist, he reached out and took his face in both hands to physically turn his head to meet his eyes. "You need to look at me; open your eyes. I can't help you if you won't even look at me."

After a couple moments of silence, he sighed and backed away. "It looks like we'll have to talk more later," he said as he moved to the next person in the semicircle of chairs. Jen had a difficult time pulling her eyes away from Bailey to see who the lousy therapist's next victim would be.

To her surprise, Jon appeared to be a lot more relaxed than the others. Because of the way the chairs were positioned, she had a better view of Jon than she had of either Zack or Bailey and she was pleasantly surprised at what she saw. His hair looked recently cut, so that it was off his shoulders, a shaggy mass of dark blonde waves. He was dressed in blue jeans and a short-sleeved shirt, as most of the people there were but unlike all of the others, he was wearing shoes that looked as though they had recently been outside. He smirked at the therapist as he approached, and Jen realized that Jon was a lot larger than she had remembered him to be. Somehow, with him dressed in street clothes and in a well-lit room, he appeared far more imposing than he had been in the shadows that had dominated the demons' lair.

Before the therapist had a chance to say anything to Jon, Bailey slumped from his chair and dropped to the floor. The therapist and Jon both reached out to catch him but Bailey shied away from both of them and crawled across the floor. Jen looked down at him in amazement as he crawled in her direction and realized that his sad, watery brown eyes were firmly locked on her own. Tears continued to drip down his cheeks as he lowered his head and sat at her feet, leaning against her and putting his head into her lap.

She reached down to smooth his hair, surprised at how soft it was now that it was clean. "It's okay," she murmured to him. "You're safe here." He didn't answer her, but Jen didn't care. She just soothed him as best she could, hoping that she was doing the right thing.

"Bailey, you know you aren't supposed to leave the circle until we're finished," the therapist's voice called over to them. At the sound, Bailey let out a whimper and fell to the ground, curling protectively into a ball at Jen's feet.

Frustrated at the therapist's apparent lack of sympathy, Jen slipped from her own chair and knelt on the floor next to Bailey. She continued to stroke his hair and speak soothingly to him but the therapist was quickly growing annoyed.

"What is she doing here? Maureen?" His voice was far louder than it had been before and there was a distinct tone of ire in it. "I left strict instructions that these sessions were not to be interrupted."

"I tried," Maureen began to explain, but the therapist cut her off.

"For that matter, they aren't to have any visitors at all. You know what kind of a precarious situation these people are in." For the first time, he looked down at Jen as he stepped closer to her. "You need to leave. There's no reason for you to be here."

"I told you not to rile them up," Maureen piped in. "And you agreed not to. That was the only reason I let you in but apparently that was too much to ask."

"Now hang on a second," Jen looked up at the pair of them. "I have permission to be here." She looked over at Maureen as she continued. "I showed you my permission when I got here."

"I don't care who gave you permission," she retorted. "You were specifically told to stay out of the way and not interfere. I'm afraid you'll have to leave."

To Jen's surprise, Jon stepped forward. "She can stay," he said as he looked between the therapist and Maureen. "She was one of the people that rescued us. We'd all still be stuck in that miserable hell-hole if it hadn't been for her."

"You're on the team that got them?" The therapist looked back at her incredulously. "All the more reason for you to leave. These people don't need to be around any more violence right now." He stepped closer, as though he was planning to bodily throw her out of the house.

As much as Jen wanted to tell them both where to stick their opinions, she looked around the room and thought better of the idea. Everyone in the gathered group was looking at her, some with expressions of surprise but a few with eyes wide in hope. Biting her tongue, she looked at each of them for a long moment. The therapist and Maureen were both speaking to her but she didn't hear a word of it.

"I just wanted to see for myself that you guys are being taken care of," she said as she ran her hand gently across Bailey's hair again. "I hadn't meant to cause any trouble when I came."

Jon shook his head, smiling down at her as he spoke. "You aren't any trouble."

She smiled back at him. "Thanks. But it looks like it was a bit of a surprise, and nobody was expecting me right now. I'll let you guys get back to your therapy and I'll be back soon, I promise."

She carefully and gently untangled herself from Bailey and stood up. Jon offered a hand to help her to her feet, which she accepted.

"Where do you think you're going?" The group's therapist called out after them as Jon led her to the front door.

"I'm walking her out, what does it look like?" He retorted before Jen could speak. "I'll be back in a minute."

"No, you get back in here. We aren't finished."

Jon spun around to face him. "The last time I checked, I wasn't in prison. I'm walking her out and I'll be right back, so you can just be patient until then."

The therapist looked as though he was going

to say more but apparently thought better of it. Maureen, however, stepped forward to escort her outside as well. "I think that it would be better if you didn't come back," she said once they were out of earshot of the rest of the group. "I knew that letting you in was a bad idea but you've seen that everyone's taken care of, so you can just go along your way."

Jen looked at the woman in surprise, not sure whether she was amused or offended. She decided once she heard Jon snickering on the other side of her. "I hope you aren't intending on scaring her off," he sneered at the woman. "I think she's about as likely to be afraid of you as I am."

Maureen shook her head. "Honestly, I don't know why you're even still here. You've done nothing but cause problems since you were brought in, and you have made it clear that you couldn't care less about the treatment program. I'm starting to wonder if you stay for the free room and board." She glared up at the large man, who simply smirked down at her.

"I stay because I'm not willing to leave these

people alone with you and Doctor Dumbass in there. Once they're ready to go, I'll go as well."

Maureen snorted and opened the door, holding it open for Jen. "Make it quick, will you? I still have to go in there and clean up the mess you've made."

Jen stifled a derisive snort and turned to hug Jon. "Thank you," she said as she wrapped her arms around him, barely even able to touch her hands across his expansive back. "I'll be back soon."

"You'd better be," he said as he held her close. "I think everyone needed to see you and it's pretty obvious that Bailey was happy to see you too."

Jen nodded against his chest. "I'm not sure when, but I'll be back as soon as I can." She let go and stepped back, and for a moment Jon seemed to hesitate before letting go as well. When she looked up at his face, she realized that there was still a lot of sadness buried behind the amusement in his eyes and she hoped that she hadn't made it worse by coming.

Without another word, she turned and

stepped out the door, shaking her head as she heard the lock click behind her.

As she climbed into her truck and pulled out onto the street, she changed her mind on which direction she wanted to go. Initially, she had intended on heading home, with maybe a stop along the way to pick up something to eat, but instead she turned toward the office. The more she thought about it, the less she liked the situation that the group was in.

She stormed into David's office, poured herself a cup of coffee, and flopped in her favorite uncomfortable chair. "Do you have any idea how awful those people are?" She took a drink of her coffee before she realized that she and David weren't alone in the office. Charlie sat in the chair next to her, one eyebrow raised at her outburst.

"Good, you're here too. I was going to ask David to talk to you anyway." She turned in her seat to face the NPIB officer more fully. "You need to do something about their therapist; that guy's terrible, and the woman who's overseeing the house they live in is even worse."

She explained how much the therapist was

pushing on the people there and how Maureen had been outright hostile towards Jon. "It's not making them better; it's going to do more damage. Poor Bailey was still in tears when I left."

Charlie leaned back, surprised at her forthrightness. "I'll have to look and see who else I can find to take over their case," he said at last, "but it might take a while."

"How long is a while?" she demanded.

"I really don't know. There haven't been a lot of cases with people who have been through that type of trauma, so there aren't many therapists who are capable of dealing with it. Until I find one that's willing and able to take care of them, Dr. Lycheck is what we've got."

Jen blinked at him for a long moment before standing up again. "That jackass is worse than having no therapy at all. He has no idea what they've been through, and he doesn't seem to give very much of a damn about finding out." She gulped down the last of her coffee and headed towards the door. "Let alone helping them work through it."

"Wait a minute," Charlie called after her before she left. "I'll look for someone else. At the very least, I should be able to find another caretaker for them. I'm not just blowing you off."

Jen stopped and looked over at him, her hand still on the door. "That'd be a good start," she admitted. "How long do you think that'll take?"

With a sigh, Charlie shrugged. "Her contract is by the month, so there's no way I can get her released until at the very least this month is over. As long as I can find someone new by then, I can get her switched out relatively easily."

Jen nodded slowly. It wasn't the unreasonably immediate result that she would have liked but at least it appeared that Charlie was willing to work with her. "Do you think you can find someone new in a couple weeks?" There wasn't very much time left in that month and Jen would rather have Maureen replaced as soon as possible instead of having to keep her for an entire month on top of that. The therapist was bad enough, but the group had to deal with Maureen on a much more frequent basis.

"Caretakers are far less specialized than therapists are, so finding a new one shouldn't be wearing lately. Not wanting to cause a fight, she simply shrugged and smiled at her parents.

Patrick was there as well, and he grinned at Jen as she tapped over to the table, barely wobbling on her dainty heels. "I take it Jaime's to blame for that?" he guessed.

Jen snickered at him. "As if I would have picked any of this stuff out for myself."

When the waiter came by, Jen ordered a drink, as did her mother. While they waited for their table, Jen watched the throngs of holiday shoppers that bustled along the street, getting ready for Yule and their last-minute gift shopping, no doubt. Although the patio was open to the street, there were heat lamps attached to the roof every few feet, so it wasn't cold.

Janice took the opportunity to ask Jen about her dating habits. "Honestly, I don't understand why you are so resistant to having any sort of normal relationship," she said as she stirred her rum and cola. "It's not that you aren't pretty, it just seems like you don't care."

"I really don't care," Jen agreed. "I don't dress like this and I have almost as much style sense as a wombat." She eyed her mother over her peach margarita. "And if I do decide to get to-gether with someone, he's just going to accept that."

Janice sighed. They had been over this same argument more times than either of them could remember, the only change was in which ani-mal Jen compared herself to. "Your sisters both pay a lot more attention to what they look like, and your father still has to beat the boys away from Mary with a stick."

"That's because Mary's a girl," Jen retorted. "And so is Jaime. Besides, it's not like any of the boys even stand a chance with Mary. As for me, I'm almost as much of a boy as Todd is." She took a sip of her drink, watching her mother cringe. "I just came out with different plumbing."

Janice leaned closer to her daughter. "You are interested in men, aren't you?" Both of her eyebrows were raised, and Jen sighed in frus-tration.

"We've been through this before," Jen re-minded her. "I'm not a lesbian and I *have* had relationships with men. I'm just not in one right now."

until firing it was almost second nature. The vampire stopped his advance to fight against the metal-woven netting and Jen knew that she didn't have very long before he managed to free himself. As he thrashed around, she drew her pistol and closed the distance between them. Wishing she had taken more target practice but not willing to let the Vamp escape, she moved in far closer than she felt safe, to a distance that she had at least a moderate amount of faith in her aim. Taking aim at his shoulder, she took a deep breath and slowly let it out, just as J.J. had taught her to, and squeezed the trigger.

The round tore through the Vamp, who screamed in a combination of pain and surprise. She put another round into his other shoulder to slow him further, praying that the team would show up soon but knowing that it was still going to be a while. Although the rounds she was using were specifically designed for dealing with this type of creature, vampires still healed far too quickly for Jen's taste. As the Vamp struggled to his feet, Jen took a step backwards to stay well outside of his reach, followed by another.

She aimed lower with her next shot, placing the round into his upper thigh. Screaming again, the vampire clutched at his wound and fell to the ground once more. He didn't stay there for long, because as soon as he hit the pavement, he started to push himself back to his feet.

Jen used his moment of distraction to move around behind him and dropped a knee in between his shoulder blades before he had completely regained his footing, this time thankful for having two brothers. Even a severely wounded Vamp was a lot stronger than she was and she knew it. "I've got one shot," she told herself as she uncapped the syringe.

She plunged the tranquilizer into the vampire's neck, pressing it in as deep as she could. Once she was sure that she couldn't press it in any further, she let go with her left hand and slammed the heel of her palm into the plunger.

As the tranquilizer flowed into the vampire's system, she could feel him start to relax but she knew better than to let him go before she was positive that he was unconscious. She knelt on top of his quickly weakening form and gripped him with both of her knees, pressing

Chapter 11

Partly because she had promised but mostly because she was eager to see them again, Jen headed down to the group home where Jon, Bailey, Zack, and all of the others were living late the next morning. She pulled up and parked at the curb in roughly the same place as she had the last time and checked to be sure that she had all of her appropriate paperwork before heading up to the house. With a scowl, she knew that Maureen would do her best to keep her out, even knowing that Jen was allowed to be there, so she needed to keep her papers on her just in case.

When she rang the bell, Maureen looked less than pleased to see her again. "I thought you weren't coming back," she commented when she recognized Jen.

Jen didn't bother to reply, simply choosing to hold up her papers. With a sigh, Maureen stepped back and allowed her to enter. "At least you aren't interrupting therapy again," she grumbled as she closed the door.

To Jen's surprise, Maureen didn't try to get in her way at all as she walked into the house. She wasn't sure what she had been expecting but she had figured that the annoying woman would try to deter her somehow. But she made it into the living room without having to argue about it.

She hadn't expected for there to be much change in the few days since her first visit and she wasn't disappointed. Zack, Bailey, Jon and Andre were all in the living room, along with Christy and a couple of the other girls that Jen hadn't ever learned the names of. Slowly and carefully, not wanting to surprise anyone, she walked across the room and took a seat on one of the long couches that had replaced the folding chairs that had been there last time.

Apparently, Zack's nudity hadn't just been

at and by the time Jen realized he had moved, Bailey was halfway to her. She stepped forward and dropped to a knee because he was crawling just as he had the last time.

Jen knew that his crawling was a direct result of the demons that had held them in their lair. Whenever they brought someone out for entertainment, the people had been led on hands and knees, attached to chain leashes with metal and leather collars around their necks. Most of the group had been in agreement that the demons had possessed Bailey for the longest amount of time before their release. No surprise, he seemed to be having the hardest time adapting to life outside of the demons' lair.

He crawled into her arms and Jen pulled him in tight to hug him. She wasn't sure why he did that every time he saw her but if that was what he needed, it was the least she could do. She smoothed his hair and ran her hands over his shoulders and upper back for a couple moments before looking up at the rest of the group.

"Bailey," Maureen called out from behind Jen,

"Dr. Lycheck told you the last time your friend was here that we don't greet people that way."

Ignoring the woman, Jen pointed out to the gathered people, "I told you guys that I'd be back."

"I know," Jon responded, ignoring Maureen as well, "but I don't think anyone was expecting you to be here so soon." He smiled down at her, and even his eyes lit up.

She couldn't help but smile in return. "How are you guys doing?"

"I'd be better if that numbskull would get out of my chair," he said, thumbing behind him to the chair that now sat vacant. Unable to see what was going on, Andre had moved and was now perched on the back of the back of the sofa.

Jen ran her hands over Bailey again before standing up. "I want to say hi to everyone else, too," she informed him when he looked up at her, hesitant to let go of her legs. "I'm not going anywhere."

Obviously reluctant, Bailey let go of her and sat back on his haunches. As she walked towards the group, he followed at her heels, unwilling to let her go too far away from him.

"Bailey," Maureen called out again, "you are supposed to walk. We don't crawl everywhere we want to go. Remember what Dr. Lycheck was talking to you about the other day?"

Jon stepped forward toward Jen, holding both arms open wide. She stepped into his embrace and squeezed him tightly, knowing that she wasn't strong enough to hurt him. Next to Jon and a few feet behind, Zack stood, silently watching and waiting. Jen turned to him next, not bothered in the slightest by his choice in apparel. She pulled the smaller man in tight also but not quite as tightly as she had done with Jon. To her surprise, Zack wrapped his arms around her as well, clutching tightly to her.

Not to be outdone, Andre hopped down from the back of the couch where he had been perched and wrapped his arms around both of them. "Group hug," he called out, which caused a small amount of snickering among the rest of the gathered people.

"Zack, that isn't appropriate. If you want to be around people like this, you need to go get some clothes on like Dr. Lycheck said." As before, everyone ignored what Maureen was saying but even Zack's lips curled up in a sneer at the sound of her voice.

Jen reached out with one arm to wrap it around Andre as well but she couldn't help but laugh. Once he and Zack let go, she made her rounds of the girls, making sure that she got a chance to hug each of them. When she was out of people in the living room, she looked back over at Jon. "Where's everyone else?"

"They were sent home," he explained. "We're the only ones left who either didn't want to go, or didn't have anywhere else to go."

"I hadn't realized that they were sending people home yet."

Jon and a few of the others shrugged. "Doctor Dumbass said that as long as everyone continued treatment wherever they went, they'd be okay to release." His expression clearly showed what he thought of that idea.

"You really need to stop calling him that," Maureen called from the other end of the room. "Dr. Lycheck's done a lot for all of you. Just because you act like it's all a big joke, there's no reason for you be snide about it."

"Nobody asked you," Jon called over without even looking up. "He sent those people out without having any real idea of what he was doing. I'll be amazed if they're all still alive in a year."

"How dare you," Maureen said as she started to step forward but Jen stepped in between them.

"Calm down," she said as she took Jon's arm. "Everything's going to be okay, I'm sure that the guy in charge will keep track of everyone, even with them spread out now."

He looked down at her in surprise. "You know him?"

"And I'll go talk to him later; just to be sure he's actually following through with that. Okay?"

He nodded, slightly mollified. After a moment, a wry smile curved the right side of his lips. "You're still trying to protect us, aren't you?"

Jen just shrugged up at him, smiling. "Aren't you doing the same thing?"

"What do you mean?"

"The last time I was here, there was some talk about you being able to leave and if the doctor's releasing people to go home, why are you still here?"

Jon snickered and thumbed over at Zack. "Because he's been one of my best friends for years, there's no way I'm leaving him here like this all alone."

Jen looked between the two men in surprise. "Really? I had no idea. I just thought you guys were stuck there like we all were."

"Nope, we got there at the same time, came in together." He explained how they had both gone to a job interview. "We think there was something in the coffee they offered us," he explained. "When we woke back up, we were in that dungeon thing."

"I answered an ad in the paper," Christy offered.

Jen blinked at him in surprise. "An ad? Like in the classifieds?"

"There was a man looking for submissives in the personal ads. I was without a master at the time, so I figured what the hell." She cast a downward glance before continuing. "I wasn't expecting what happened afterwards."

Jen blinked at her in confusion. "What's a submissive? And why would you answer an ad like that?"

Now it was Christy's turn to look at her in surprise. "You didn't know?" When she shook her head, she explained. "There are two kinds of people in that lifestyle, the dominant ones, or doms; they're the bosses and they control everything. On the other side are the submissives, or subs, which are expected to do whatever the dom demands and in return they are taken care of."

"And this was something you knew about before going over there?"

"Sort of. Anna here," she gestured to the dark-skinned girl, "had been in it a lot longer than I have, I'd only just started experimenting with it. But we both enjoyed it, and I wanted to try more, so we went for it."

"I didn't know that there were people who liked that kind of thing," Jen said, still trying to sort out what she was hearing. "I thought you guys had all been caught like I had been."

"We didn't realize until a lot later that you weren't there for the same reasons we were. Honestly, at first, I thought you just liked the beatings."

Jen looked at her, appalled. "Liked the beatings? How could anyone like those?"

"I do," Andre spoke up. "That was how I ended up there." He grinned between her and the two men. "Granted, I don't like to be beaten as far as they liked to beat us, but there wasn't really much controlling them about it."

Jen turned her confused expression towards him. "Are you serious?"

Andre nodded, his grin widening. "I got picked up in a club," he explained. "There was this seriously hot woman there that came on to me, asked me to come home with her for a little slap-and-tickle. Now, I'm always game for some of that, so I agreed." His grin faltered for a moment as he thought. "I don't really remember much after that, the next thing I knew, I was strapped to a table with the demons and the woman wasn't there anymore." He looked over at Jen and winked. "Then you came in."

Jen felt her face redden as she remembered

that day. "But... you were crying," she protested. "How can you say you enjoyed it when you were crying?"

"Because it hurt," he laughed but only for a moment before sobering again. "But I could tell that you weren't enjoying it and that was when I realized that there was something wrong."

"There was a lot wrong there," Zack spoke up for the first time, but he kept his eyes downcast.

"At least for most people there was," Andre added. "I like pain, so a good whipping's a pretty good thing for me but not even I can take that much for very long."

"Yeah, but you're a masochist," Jon explained. "And for people who aren't into pain like Andre is, beatings are a bad thing."

"What's a masochist?" Jen asked, thoroughly confused. This group seemed to know so many words that she was unfamiliar with, it felt like being back in high school literature class.

"Someone who likes pain," Andre answered. "I'm not so much into being submissive in everything but I'm definitely into some good beatings from time to time."

"And that's what you thought you were getting into?" Jen asked, looking around the group. She would have said more, but her phone started to ring. Swearing, she flipped it open. "Hey, Marc. What's up?"

"Your psychic's at it again," he said. "We're getting geared to head out. How soon can you get here?"

Jen swore again and checked her watch. "I'm not even close to the office, so it'll take me a while."

"Are you close to 53rd and Hewlett?"

"A lot closer than I am to the office. I'll get geared up on the way. What's he up to this time?"

"I'll explain on the scene. If you arrive before we do, just stay down until we get there, okay?"

As Jen hung up the phone, she looked apologetically at the group. "I have to go."

Jon waved her off. "You go do what you have to do. We'll be here when you come again."

"Take care of them until then," she called over to him as she jogged for the door.

Chapter 12

Thaxter sat at a coffee shop just down the street, within sight of the house that now held a large number of the people who had until recently been his prized possessions. He sipped at a cup of coffee and nibbled at a scone, watching the house carefully. Jen had been inside for only a short while and he was curious about why she continued to go back there. As far as he could tell, she wasn't being forced to go, yet still she returned every few days.

As he pondered, a woman walked over to the table, carrying her own cup of coffee. She was tall, as most succubi were, with rich auburn hair that flowed past her shoulders, deep emerald eyes, and a pair of dimples in each cheek. "I have news," she said as she sat across the table from him and took a sip of her coffee.

"What's that?" he asked without looking away from the window.

"The Inquisitors have heard about what happened at the lair and they aren't happy about it."

"No big surprise, Mariette," Thaxter answered as he took another bite of his pastry. He tore his gaze away from the window to look at his companion. "I knew as soon as I found out Vanitha had been captured that they were going to be angry."

"You've been removed from your position," she continued. "I'm not sure who will be chosen to replace either you or Vanitha but I'd wager that it'll happen soon."

Thaxter took a drink of his coffee and turned back to the window.

Mariette sighed. "Apparently Maddock's the angriest of all the Inquisitors. He's said that he holds you personally responsible for losing the woman." She evaluated her partner before continuing but there was no sign of reaction. "He says that if you had done your job correctly in the first place, she wouldn't be running free and able to cause more trouble for them."

The incubus just shrugged and took another sip of his coffee. Inwardly, he was seething. How dare they blame him for what had happened? None of the Inquisitors had any idea about how many safety precautions he had taken in order to ensure that Jen couldn't escape. In fact, he wasn't entirely sure himself how her team had managed to cross the barrier to his world; his magic should have been more than strong enough to hold back even the most powerful of mages.

Above and beyond that, he still wanted to know what Maddock's fascination with Jen had been. Or continued to be, he corrected himself. As far as he could tell, the Inquisitor hadn't made any moves toward capturing her again but it was only a matter of time.

Unwittingly, the succubus confirmed his suspicions. "It'll all be taken care of soon, though. Apparently, there's someone else that's out for her, someone that the Inquisitors believe will do a better job." She took a drink of her coffee and smiled pleasantly. "Maybe this one will be able to kill her, since you couldn't seem to bring yourself to do it."

The rise she had expected to get out of Thaxter barely showed. He lowered his eyebrows minutely and glowered at her through iron-cold eyes but said nothing. Exasperated, she set her cup back onto the table with an audible thump, splashing a small amount of her beverage onto the polished wood table.

"I really don't see why you were so insistent on getting her to accept you as her master, instead of just killing her like they wanted you to. You hadn't expected her to just give in to you, did you?"

Thaxter shrugged. "I really don't know. There's something different about her, something I still can't quite place but I want to know what it is."

"Is that why you're stalking her now?" She asked as she looked past him through the window. They could both see Jen as she left the house and jogged out to the street, where her Jeep was parked. With a roar of the engine and a shriek of tires, the woman shot down the street in a large, square, emerald green bullet.

"Seems to me like you could find plenty more of interest here to fixate on. I don't see why you find this single human so fascinating."

"Maybe you're right," Thaxter shrugged and took another drink of his coffee. To his dismay, he discovered that his cup had run dry, so with a sigh he stood and headed for the door. "Thank you for your information," he said as he sauntered toward the door. "I will be in touch if I need anything else."

Chapter 13

Jen turned on Hewlett, heading for 53rd. This attack was a lot closer to her house than the last attack by the psychic had been and Jen wondered if that was because of his admission that he was specifically after her. Even though she wasn't at her house when she got the call, she was still a lot closer to him than the rest of the team was, so none of them had arrived by the time she got there. The fact that she drove like the proverbial bat out of hell didn't help much either.

She had to stop fairly soon after turning the corner because there were damaged trucks, cars, and even the occasional minivan littering the street and adjoining yards. She pulled to the edge of the road and turned off the truck before carefully climbing out onto the icy street. A cold wind blew across her face as she turned to survey the damage and she reached back into the Jeep to retrieve her jacket. It was a lot warmer inside with the heater but there wasn't a lot she could do about Old Man Winter's domain. Jen changed into her armor, wondering why there were so many people who looked forward to the cold weather. Once she was ready to go, she pulled her shotgun out of its locked rack and hefted it to her shoulder. Along with the gun, she pulled a handful of tranquilizers out of their case and dropped them into a pocket. With a sigh, she stepped into the carnage in search of the source.

Flipped cars were sprawled everywhere on the street; others landed in household yards, creating deep scars in the snow-covered, frozen ground. A handful of people had escaped from the wrecks and were simply trying to escape the psychic's rampage but others were too badly injured to move very far. Jen stopped at the first few people she came to, partly to make sure that they were still alive and to re-assure them that help was coming. It also gave her an extra couple of precious minutes to look around, surveying the damage and trying to formulate a plan.

Houses had been attacked as well, she discovered as she looked around. The damage seemed to be mainly focused on the garages, where doors had been blasted open. It appeared to Jen as though the attacker was looking for something without knowing exactly where it was. The main bulk of the houses hadn't remained untouched, however, as a few of them had been severely damaged as well. The residents of the damaged houses appeared to have been left mostly unhurt and some were trying to help the people who had been wounded in the attack.

More explosions sounded ahead and Jen left the handful of residents who were helping to take care of the injured. "There's a response team on the way," she called over to one of the good Samaritans. "Just hang in there."

When she got to the end of the next block, she spotted the psychic immediately, mostly because he was making no attempt to hide himself. He was calmly walking down the street into oncoming traffic, blasting at cars as he went with his blue and gold energy attacks. There were even more wrecks all over the place there, much as there had been when he had made his attack on the highway.

She jogged ahead, pulling out her phone and calling Marc as she went. "Looks like the same guy, all right." She described what was going on and how similar it was to the psychic's last attack. "I sure hope there are ambulances coming, too. There's a lot of wounded out here."

"Yeah, there are," Marc reassured her. "But you need to wait for us before you get too close to him."

Ahead, she could hear more people screaming and she decided that caution simply wouldn't work. "Dammit, there are more people up there; I've got to see if I can get them out."

Marc answered her but she couldn't hear any of it because her phone had snapped shut as she dropped it into her pocket. She moved closer to the commotion, drawing her pistol from its holster as she went. As much as she would love to open fire with the shotgun, it still sounded as though there were too many people ahead for her to get a clean shot without fear of hitting the passersby as well. She ducked behind a wrecked car for cover, realizing that it wasn't the best cover she could get against a psychic but it was the best she had. The little blue sports car had probably been nice before the attack, she noticed offhandedly. One of her old neighbors had owned one and she briefly wondered if it was the same car.

She peeked around the car's trunk and visually confirmed that it was indeed the same psychic as before. There weren't any people in sight but Jen could hear the sound of them in the area. He continued down the street in the same direction he had been heading before her arrival and, as she watched, he blasted a hole in another person's house. Screaming from inside the residence joined the cacophony outside and Jen knew she had to do something before more people got hurt.

"Is that you again, dumbass?" She called to him over the car, taking care to stay low enough to remain mostly hidden. Only inches off the ground, she peeked around the car and aimed her pistol at him. She didn't have the best angle she could have hoped for and the pistol was by far not her strongest weapon but it was the best she had right then.

She just hoped it would be enough.

As he turned toward her voice, she popped a couple of rounds at him. As it did every time, the kick from the pistol tugged her aim off and she winced to herself, hoping that it hadn't thrown her aim too far off, wasting the only advantage she had.

The bullets surprised him and he didn't have any defenses in place, so one of the rounds hit its mark. Jen swore as she saw that, vowing again that she needed to spend a lot more time at the range. *At least the round that had missed him was too high to have hit anyone else*, she told herself silently as she prepared to fire again.

Even as she got ready to release the second pair of bullets, the psychic bent down. At first, Jen thought he was ducking and moving for cover, so she prepared to move as well. She couldn't tell if he knew where she was but her cover wouldn't work for very much longer. Either way, she looked around for another place to move and take her next shots from. When he stood back up, however, she realized that the situation was far worse than she had expected.

He hauled a woman up in front of him and Jen swore as she realized what he was up to. His hostage looked to be almost seventy years old and a part of her hoped that she was a Were, even though she knew that the likelihood of that was somewhere between slim and none. The old woman shrieked as he lifted her off the ground and even at the distance she watched from Jen could see the terrified tears streaming down the elderly woman's face. She was wearing the type of dress that Jen's grandmother had always referred to as a housecoat, shapeless panels of fabric and a simple pair of slippers. Jen could only guess that the woman had come out of one of the neighboring houses to administer some sort of aid and now she was caught right in the middle of the mess.

He grinned in Jen's direction, one of the most evil-looking smirks that she had seen in a long while, and began advancing toward her. "There you are," he said as he moved closer. "I was wondering how long it would take before you showed up." He raised his left hand, while still using his right to hold the woman close against him and pointed at her. "I've been waiting a long time for this."

As the energy bolt blasted out from his outstretched hand and shot toward her, Jen dove from behind the car. She didn't have a clear plan to where she was moving but she knew that if she didn't start moving, and fast, she was dead. Perhaps waiting for her team hadn't been such a bad idea after all, but it was far too late to do anything about it now.

"What do you want with me?" she called over the explosion as the energy blast hit the car she had just vacated, sending fragments of blue-painted fiberglass everywhere. To make matters worse, it appeared that the psychic had grown stronger since his last attack, because that blast was a lot larger and apparently more powerful than the ones he had used at the restaurant. "If it really is me you're after, leave these people alone!"

"I don't think so," he replied as he sent another bolt in her direction. "If it wasn't for you, he wouldn't have abandoned me." The explosion barely missed Jen, flying only inches over her as she threw herself to the ground and rolled behind yet another smashed car. "But I was supposed to kill you and I failed. He won't come back until you're dead." She couldn't see him from the position she had landed in but she was sure that he was preparing to unleash another burst of energy.

"Who are you talking about?" she called as she peeked around the car to see where he had moved to. To her relief, the psychic had dropped his hostage and Jen could see the frightened woman crawling away from him as fast as she could move. One of her slippers lay forgotten in the middle of the street, a hump of muddy cloth. Jen breathed a sigh of relief to see that the hostage was out of danger now but the psychic was readying another blast. She dropped to the ground again and scurried to get to another position before he caught up with her.

She scrambled behind a large decorative ceramic pot that someone had placed in their front yard. There had once been a large, flowering bush in it but now there were just a few straggled branches scattered across the ground and fresh chips in the edge of the pot, obvious signs that it had taken at least some damage already in the madman's attack. She sat with her back to it, holding her pistol to her chest and praying that she could get a clear shot on the crazed man before he did any more damage, killed her, or snagged another hostage.

"He's powerful," the psychic called out to her. "Far more powerful than any person could ever hope to be. But then, he's a demon and demons are always more powerful than humans, you know."

Jen's eyes widened in surprise at his mention of demons. "Is this about Cylin?" she called out as she peeked over the top edge of the pot. The psychic wasn't quite in view, but from the proximity of his voice, she could tell that he had gotten a lot closer. Since Cylin was dead, it would make sense for his psychic follower to believe he had been abandoned. Although Jen hadn't killed him herself, he had been killed because of her. She wasn't about to feel guilty over it, however. That sadistic bastard had deserved to die.

"Cylin?" The psychic called back as another

blast exploded on the ground near her. "I don't know who that is. I'm talking about Maddock."

As she left the dying tree and the pot that held it behind and moved to her next cover, Jen wondered who Maddock was. Just as she ducked behind an overturned pickup truck, her radio crackled to life. "We're at your truck," Marc's voice called out. "Where are you?"

Jen swore and tried to dive from behind the truck, but she couldn't move quickly enough. The explosion rocked the truck and rolled it towards her. She dropped to all fours, intent on scampering away as quickly as she could but the belt loop of her pants caught on the torn metal of the truck's door. The truck was being shoved toward her even as it rolled over onto her and, knowing that there was nowhere left to run, she knelt on the frozen pavement and bent double, covering her head with her arms.

She could feel the crumpled metal of the truck's door press against her but then, suddenly, the pressure stopped. She cracked an eye, surprised and wondering why she hadn't just been turned into a pancake.

To her amazement, standing over her and

holding the truck from flattening her was Thaxter.

He reached down and took her by the arm, hefting her to her feet. Jen saw energy blasts hitting the incubus, one after another, but they just seemed to absorb into him as soon as they hit. He ignored the blasts and picked Jen up, ripping her snagged belt loop free in the process, before stepping away from the destroyed truck.

With a wave of a hand, he opened a portal that looked just like the one he had used when he took Jen to Derathim. As she realized what was about to happen, Jen screamed, kicking out and beating on him in a panicked attempt to escape. His arms around her felt like steel bands and she knew that there was no way she could force him to release her, but she had to try.

The psychic, also recognizing what was about to happen and not about to let his prey escape, let loose another volley of energy blasts, which were quickly weakening as he ran out of power. "NO!" He screamed at the demon. "She was tasked to me; you can't take her!" He charged at the portal as though he intended to either stop them from passing through it or to follow them.

Thaxter absorbed all of the bolts as easily as he had the first and, ignoring the ineffective fight Jen was putting up, the demon stepped into the portal. She shrieked again as she felt the same wrenching sensation as before and in only seconds they were out the other side. Her eyes squeezed shut, Jen couldn't immediately tell where they were but she had her suspicions. Her worst nightmare was about to come true.

The demon took a couple of steps before releasing his grip on her and dropping her onto something... soft? She bounced, not very high but the sensation alone was enough to shock her eyes open. Neither the dungeon nor the darkroom had anything that could be considered soft.

She was sprawled on a bed, but it wasn't just any bed. She was in her own house and the demon had dropped her onto her own bed. She looked around the room, confused and surprised, before looking back up at the incubus. She rolled off the bed and onto the floor as far away from the demon as she could go but there weren't many places where she could run. He stood between her and the door, so the only option she had left for escape would be out the window. She wasn't looking forward to the two-story jump but at least the snow would cushion her landing slightly.

Almost as though he knew her intentions, he was at her side before she had taken two steps toward the window. He grabbed her by the shoulder and pushed her against the wall, not hard enough to hurt her but forcefully enough that she had to move her feet backwards to keep them beneath her in case he let go. He held her in place with his body, pressing himself against her and moving his hand from her shoulder to the wall next to her head.

"Stupid woman," he growled down at her. "I save your life and the first thing you do is try to jump out a window?"

She looked up at him in surprise. She wasn't sure why he had brought her back to her house instead of back to his lair but she was relieved, no matter what his reasons were. "What are you going to do to me?" She hadn't intended to ask but she needed to know.

"Keep you from doing something idiotic, apparently," he replied. As he looked down at her, Jen was surprised to discover that there was no real anger in his eyes, only irritation.

The quip that she had been about to release stalled in her throat as she thought better about her actions. Instead, she reached up slowly and put both of her palms against his chest. Her heart racing and wondering how badly he was about to hurt her for what she was doing, she pressed outwards to push him off of her.

To her surprise, he backed away, but only his upper body and only far enough to let her breathe more easily. His hands were still planted on the wall on either side of her, his leg pressed tight against her. She knew that there was no way she could get past him; she had barely even seen him move as he came after her, he had just seemed to appear in front of her.

"You seem to have forgotten," he said to her. "You belong to me."

Jen shook her head, wondering why he hadn't tried to hit her yet. "No, I don't. I never belonged to you." She made sure to keep her voice low and steady, not wanting to irritate the demon any more than she already had.

His eyes darkened as she spoke but his hands stayed where they were. "Still you deny me?" His gaze lowered from her face and down her body. She could feel her body react as he watched, and somehow, she knew that he was responsible. Vaguely, she remembered that he had done this to her once before, while she had still been his captive.

Before she realized what she was doing, she pushed out with all of her strength, shoving the demon away from her. "Get out of my head!" she exclaimed.

He stumbled backward, an expression of surprise on his face. "How dare you?" he asked as he stepped closer again. "You destroy my home, you kill my protégé, and still you continue to defy me." He took her by the shoulders again and held her, this time at arm's length as he glared at her. "Do you have any idea what you've done?"

"I don't care," she retorted. "What about what you've done? You kidnap people, beat them and abuse them in any way you can. Have you thought about that?"

He snickered at her outburst, not the reaction she had expected. "Had I not taken you, you would have been dead long ago."

"What's that supposed to mean?"

"I was to have killed you," he explained. "When you were handed over to me, I was to turn your body over to the Inquisitors so that they could be assured of your death.

"Instead, I decided that you would become much more valuable as my plaything and so I kept you." He let go of her and turned towards the door. "Perhaps that was not the best decision to have made, for now you have destroyed everything." He looked back over his shoulder at her as he stepped through the door and into the hall.

"The next time I come to see you, I expect you to be more appreciative."

As the door closed behind him, Jen stepped back and slumped against the wall. She sank to the floor, confused about what had just happened and relieved that the demon had left. Although she hadn't been shaking while Thaxter had been holding her, she realized that she was trembling now. With unsteady hands, she pulled out her phone and called Marc.

"Where are you?" he answered as soon as it had started to ring. "We heard you scream but you were gone by the time we caught up."

"I'm..." she started to say before her voice faltered. "I'm at home." Despite her attempts at bravery, she couldn't hide the fear in her voice.

"At home?" he echoed. "How did you get there?" Without waiting for her to answer, he continued. "Are you okay?"

"I think so," she answered. "Could you have someone get my truck for me?"

"Yeah," he agreed, and she could hear him shouting over to someone else. "We'll be there soon. You just sit tight until we get there."

As soon as she hung up the phone, Jen searched around her room for something that she could use as a weapon. She kicked herself for her decision to not keep any weapons in her bedroom and determined that she would change that immediately.

By the time the team arrived, Jen had calmed down a bit. She had searched the house and there was no sign of the demon anywhere. Marc was the first one to arrive and he stepped into the living room slowly, as Jen was sitting on Troy's recliner, still wild-eyed, her backup pistol gripped tightly in both hands and pointed at the entryway.

Marc raised his hands. "Hey, it's us." When she lowered the weapon, he signaled to the rest of the team behind him and walked closer. He moved slowly and stepped carefully, as did the rest of the men behind him.

Although she had lowered the angle of the gun, Jen kept a tight grip on it, wide-eyed and waiting to be sure that it was only the people who were supposed to be there who were walking into the house. She knew that she wasn't being rational, but she didn't care.

"What happened?" Marc asked as he stepped closer.

"It was Thaxter," she responded without taking her eyes off the entryway. "He was here."

"The demon?" J.J. stepped closer. "What did he do? Do we need to take you to the hospital?"

Jen shook her head, finally looking up at her team. "He didn't hurt me." She looked from

Mark to J.J. and then to Ty and Mike, who were still standing in the entryway. She felt fresh tears start to slip down her cheeks but didn't move to wipe them away.

J.J. dropped his rifle, which slipped down its sling and hung at his hip. He stepped directly in front of Jen and reached down to take the pistol out of her hands. Setting it on the table next to her, he gently took her by the hands and pulled her to her feet. "Come on," he said. "We need to get you checked out, just to be sure."

Numbly, she followed him out of the house and to the waiting vehicles. She barely even noticed that her truck was there, parked in its usual spot in the driveway. Vaguely, she won-dered which of the guys had driven it, but it wasn't important enough for her to care.

J.J. walked her over to the truck that he shared with Mike and opened the passenger door for her. He helped her climb inside and climbed in after her, helping her move so that she was safely placed in between the men as Mike stepped into the driver's seat. Behind them, Marc and Ty had their truck started and soon they were in a small caravan heading down the street, headed for the hospital.

By the time they arrived at the hospital, Jen was starting to come up out of her stupor. "I'm okay, really," she protested as the guys pulled her out of the truck. "I'm not hurt, I was just scared."

"We know that," J.J. nodded affably as he tugged her off of the truck's seat, "but you're getting checked out anyway."

Apparently someone had let David know what was going on because he met them at the front door, with Dr. McAdam standing next to him. Without saying a word, Dr. McAdam reached out and took Jen by the arm, leading her into a vacant room.

"Want to tell me what happened?" he asked as he pulled a box of tissues out of a cupboard and handed them over. Although Jen had stopped crying, she could still feel how damp her cheeks were.

She pulled a couple of sheets from the box and wiped the moisture away. "I'm not hurt," she explained. "The guys just thought I was."

Dr. McAdam tilted his head at her sympathetically. "They also said that it was the same demon that had been holding you earlier."

Jen nodded, her eyes downcast. "I thought he was going to take me away again." She looked up at the doctor and wadded the soggy tissues in her hand before explaining what had transpired.

He sat and listened as she spoke, nodding occasionally. When she was finished, he stood up and stepped closer to her. "I can see how that was pretty hard for you," he said. "So I'm just going to give you a quick once-over to make sure that everything's good, okay?" When she agreed, he warned her, "I'll be running some energy tests, too, so be warned."

Jen could feel his power wash over and through her, but it didn't last for very long. Much sooner than she had expected, he took his seat again and made a couple of notes in her file. "Looks like everything's good," he said as he capped his pen. "You have a couple of minor scrapes and bruises, but nothing too bothersome."

"Great," she said with false bravado as she

hopped down from the examination table. "I'm sure the guys'll be happy to hear that too."

He followed her out into the hall, where her team was waiting anxiously. As they approached, everyone stood up to hear the news. "She's fine," Dr. McAdam said to them as soon as they were within speaking distance. "Just a little stressed out over what happened, nothing her therapist won't be able to help her with."

Jen looked down again and examined her toes. "About that..." she said. As everyone looked over at her in surprise, she looked up at them and shrugged. "He was a jerk."

"You fired him?" David asked. "When were you planning to tell me about this?"

"When I found a new one," she shrugged.

David just shook his head. "We'll talk about this at the office." He shook Dr. McAdam's hand and thanked him for treating her on such short notice.

"Don't worry about it," he waved him off. "That's what I'm here for."

David led them out to the parking lot but when Jen tried to follow Mike and J.J. over to their truck, he took her by the arm and led her over to his own car. "You're riding with me," he explained. "One of them will give you a ride home but we need to have a talk."

With a growing sense of apprehension, Jen climbed into the car with him. "You're part of a team," he said as they pulled out of the garage. "You need to start acting like it."

"But..." She started to protest, but David raised a hand to silence her.

"It's not just for your own safety, although that's quickly becoming a much larger issue. It's because when you run ahead, the team doesn't have any idea where you are or what's going on and they can't act effectively if they don't know where you are."

Jen sat in silence, not wanting to make it any worse by offering any explanations.

He sighed as he looked over at her. "I know that you're used to being on your own and you certainly seem to believe that you can do everything by yourself but even you have to admit that isn't the case. Look at what happened today."

"But I..."

"No buts," he interrupted her again. "You

were specifically told to wait for the rest of the team to arrive, weren't you?"

Lowering her head, Jen nodded.

"Do you want me to tell you about the call I got from Marc, when they showed up to hear you screaming somewhere in the distance? And then, when they got to where you should have been, both you and the psychic you were fighting with were gone? Everyone thought you'd been captured again."

"I'm sorry," Jen said in a quiet voice. "I hadn't meant to scare everyone."

"I know you hadn't," David admitted, "you were just off doing your Lone Ranger impersonation again and it needs to stop." As they pulled into the New World Response office parking lot, he glanced over at her and sighed. "So what happened with the therapist?"

Jen shrugged. "He basically told me that I had imagined the whole thing after getting high and going off for an orgy."

He looked over at her in amazement. "He said that?"

"Not in so many words, but yeah." She

glanced over at him. "I'll find another one; I just haven't found any I liked yet."

He sighed again as he pulled into his designated parking spot. "You have two weeks," he said and turned off the ignition. "If you haven't found one you like by then, I'll have to find another one for you myself."

"Okay," she agreed as she stepped out of the car.

They walked into the building in silence, and before David headed upstairs, he turned back to her. "I *am* glad that you're okay," he said. "The guys weren't the only ones who were worried about you." He looked beyond her, where Jen could hear the rest of the team entering the building. "And I believe you all have reports to write, I'm expecting them on my desk by five." Without another word, he turned and stepped into the waiting elevator.

Chapter 14

By the time she got home that night, it was a lot later than she had intended. J.J. gave her a lift home since her Jeep was still at her house and Jen had to fight from falling asleep on the drive. For some reason, she was completely exhausted and she wasn't entirely sure why. Part of her suspected that it was because of the stress of the day but another part believed that it was because she hadn't been sleeping well at night again.

"See you tomorrow?" J.J. asked as he pulled up in front of her place.

Jen opened the door. "He didn't suspend me, he just wanted to yell at me a bit."

"That's good," he laughed as she stepped

out of the truck. "Life would be kind of boring without you around, you know."

Jen had to chuckle as well. As always, J.J. always knew what to say to cheer her up. "Thanks," she said as she closed the door behind her and turned to head inside.

Troy and Patrick were both home as she walked in, busily engrossed in their nightly video game wars. Patrick paused as soon as he noticed her there, looking up at her in anticipation. "Where were you?" he asked. "Your truck was here when I got home but you weren't."

"I caught a ride with the guys," she explained. "We just finished writing up our reports, so J.J. brought me home.

Troy snickered. "Did they decree that your driving was a public menace or something?"

Jen chuckled in return and shook her head. "No, it was just a little hectic. Is there any food?"

"Yeah, we made spaghetti," Patrick called after her as she wandered towards the kitchen. "And I put your gun back into the drawer; you left it out on the table."

"Did I?" Jen glanced back over her shoulder,

vaguely remembering that she had pulled her backup pistol out of its drawer. "I was wondering where I put that." The aroma of hot, spicy spaghetti sauce reminded her stomach that she hadn't eaten since breakfast, and it began to protest loudly. Inhaling the aroma, she pulled a plate out of the cupboard and scooped an enormous serving of noodles and sauce out of the pot. "This smells delicious," she commented as she walked back out to the living room to eat.

Despite her attempts to act casual, she hadn't managed to fool either of the guys. They hadn't gone back to their game as she had expected them to. Instead, they both sat on the floor, staring at her expectantly. "Want to tell us what's really going on?" Patrick finally asked.

With a sigh, Jen sat on the couch behind them. She took a bite of her dinner, buying herself some time to think before answering. "Today was kind of rough," she admitted after swallowing. She explained about the attack by the psychic, and about how Thaxter had inexplicably come to her rescue. As both of the men popped to their feet, she waved them down with a spaghetti-loaded fork. "I'm fine, he didn't try anything," she explained. "But the guys wanted to get me checked out, just to be sure. After that, I had to finish my reports, and now I have two weeks to find a new therapist before I get in trouble over that, too." She shoved the fork into her mouth, as if to emphasize the point.

"Weren't you already looking for a new shrink?" Troy asked.

"Sorta," she shrugged in response. "I hadn't exactly been making it a priority though." She took another bite of her food before continuing. "I'd mostly been looking for a new therapist for the others that were there, too. But that's changed, too."

"How's that?" Patrick asked.

"I was looking at what happened to them as though it was the same thing that happened to me, but that wasn't right, either." She explained about how most of the people that had been held by the demons had been willing participants in the activity, at least in part. "They liked doing that kind of thing before they were taken," she looked over at the men as she took another bite. "So that changes things a bit."

Patrick looked appropriately appalled, but

Troy just looked thoughtful. "You know," he said, "I dated a girl a while ago that was into that stuff, too." He set down his controller and turned to face her more directly. "I can't say that I understand exactly where they're coming from in all this, but I do remember that there's this guy who specialized in people who'd been abused by their partners. He's pretty active in the bondage community, so I think that's why he specialized in it."

Jen looked at the hybrid in amazement. "There really are people who specialize in this?" she asked. "I had just thought that was wishful thinking on my part."

"I can make a few calls and see what I can come up with. Like I said, this was a while ago, so it might take some time to track him down but I can give it a shot."

"That'd be awesome," Jen exclaimed. She shoveled more of her dinner onto her fork and grinned. "Seriously, that's the best news I've gotten today."

She slept fitfully that night, as she had every night since returning home. As usual, she woke about an hour before the sun came up and decided that there was no point in trying to fool herself into believing that she could get back to sleep. Instead, she got up and padded downstairs in search of coffee.

She spent the next few hours in the kitchen, drinking coffee and doodling on the back of a receipt that she had found on the counter. When Patrick got up to get ready for work, he was surprised to see her. "You're up awfully early, aren't you?" he asked as he padded into the kitchen, barefoot and dressed in a pair of blue and black striped pajama pants.

"How are you?" she asked. "I haven't seen that much of you lately."

"I'm good," he answered as he poured himself a cup of coffee and leaned against the counter to take a sip. "The build is getting closer to completion and it even looks like we're coming in on budget."

"That's great," she said as she walked over towards him to refill her own cup. "And what about after it's done? What's going to happen then?"

He shook his head and shrugged, looking troubled at the question. "I guess I'll be heading out to the next site," he answered finally. He took another drink of his coffee and scowled at his cup. "I wish I could stick around for longer, if for no other reason than to make sure that you're going to be okay."

Jen waved his concern off. "I'll be fine, so don't worry about me. I was just wondering if you'd gotten any word on where you were going to be relocated to next."

"Not yet. We probably won't know that until this build's done." He drained the last of his coffee and set the empty cup into the sink. "But I'd better go get my shower before Furball gets up and hogs all the hot water."

Jen snickered as she watched her brother walk out of the room. "It's strange," she thought to herself as she took another drink from her own cup. "When he first got here, it was so strange having him around." Now she could barely even imagine him being gone. Trying to shake it off, she turned to the coffeepot again and refilled her cup.

Hearing the water start upstairs, a mischievous smile crossed her face as she turned to the sink and turned on the cold water. The yelp that came from upstairs told her that she had timed it correctly and the swearing that followed was colorful enough that she decided she would have to remember it for future use.

Once both Patrick and Troy had left for the day, Jen decided that it was her turn to go get a shower herself. In the bathroom, she pulled the pistol out of the back waistband of her pajamas and set it on the counter while she started the water running. Before she stepped under the spray, she dropped the weapon into one of the drawers just beneath the counter top and moved the can of repellant into the shower, setting it on the high shelf where she normally kept her shampoo.

She told herself that she wasn't being paranoid as she stepped under the water. Thaxter definitely knew where she lived and if he was watching, he would know that she was there alone. She wasn't willing to live the rest of her life in fear of the demon but she wasn't going to play the helpless victim, either.

After she was clean and had yet another cup of caffeine in her system, she headed out to her truck, her pistol securely placed in the shoulder holster that Troy had helpfully loaned to her until she could pick one up of her own. She surveyed the neighborhood carefully as she started the truck but there was nothing visibly amiss. Shaking her head again, she turned onto the main street and headed for Sugar and Spice.

Sahara was there, as Jen had expected but there was another woman behind the counter as well. As Jen walked in, Sahara grinned broadly and waved her over to meet her new assistant. "Jen, this is Shauna Gray. She knows a lot more about online sales than I do, so she's going to be helping me with that."

Shauna was tall, even taller than Jen. She had short, light brown hair, silvery grey eyes, and a wide frame that comfortably held a few extra pounds. She was dressed in a green long-sleeved shirt with three buttons at the neck, blue jeans, and red sneakers. Her smile was friendly and Jen quickly found herself smiling in return.

She stepped forward to shake Shauna's hand. "Nice to meet you," she said.

"I'll let you do your thing," Shauna said to Sahara. "I'll be in the back doing mine, if you need anything." With another nod to Jen, she stepped behind the wall of hanging beads that served as a barrier between the storefront and Sahara's office.

"She seems nice," Jen commented as soon as she was gone.

"She's a godsend. I was starting to get swamped with the online sales but then Joel came home and said he knew someone who had done a lot of them. He sent her over yesterday and she's already started to make improvements." She walked over to the ever-present teapot and poured herself a cup, holding up another cup at Jen questioningly. When she nodded, she poured some tea for her as well. "But enough of that, how have you been doing?"

Jen accepted the cup and stepped over to one of the shelves. She pulled down one of the jars that she had helped Sahara re-label not long ago, which was marked *"Dreamless."* She set the jar soundlessly onto the counter and took a sip of her tea.

"Nightmares again?" Sahara asked her. "Or are you trying to reach the dreamwalker?"

Jen shook her head. "Nightmares, that's all."

A short time ago, when Jen had been plagued by nightmares, Sahara had given her an herbal remedy that would eliminate her dreams. As soon as she had started taking the mixture, Steve Jenkins, the dreamwalker, had begun paying visits to her while she was sleeping. For a while, Jen had been convinced that the tea allowed the psychic to contact her and had insisted on keeping a stash of it on hand.

"That's good," Sahara said as she portioned out doses of the herbal mixture. "Because it's so much easier, not to mention cheaper, to just call him." She looked over at her friend and evaluated her for a moment. "Speaking of which, have you talked to him lately?"

"Not in the last week or so but we've talked on the phone a few times. He seems to be doing pretty well."

Sahara finished packaging Jen's order and set it on the counter. While Jen put the jar back onto its shelf, the store's phone rang. Sahara answered it cheerfully but as Jen turned back towards her, she discovered that she had gone pale. "Hang on," she said into the phone. "What's the address there?" She pulled a piece of paper off the register and jotted down the address that she had been given and waved the paper at Jen. "Go, hurry," she said as Jen took the scrap. "It's Bobby."

Without waiting for any further explanation, Jen bolted for the door. Bobby was one of Sahara's regular customers, a werewolf who was vegetarian while he was in his human form. Because of that, he came into the store every time there was a full moon, just like clockwork, to get a remedy for the inevitable stomachache. Jen had known him almost as long as Sahara had because he stopped in plenty of times between the lunar events as well. Whatever was wrong with him, Jen would try her best to help.

She glanced down at the address that Sahara had given her, surprised to see that it was only a couple of miles from the store. Spitting loose gravel as she went, Jen launched out into traffic.

Only seconds after she pulled out of the parking lot, her phone rang. "What happened to him?" She asked, not bothering to check the caller ID.

"He popped," Sahara explained.

Popped was what most werewolves referred to as shifting shape without intending to, so Jen knew that whatever she was in for, it would be bad. "Why?"

"I don't know. That was his wife on the phone; she said he just lost control."

"Okay," Jen answered. "Call my team and let them know, okay?" Jen was pretty sure that she was about to get into trouble with David again, particularly after the talking-to she had just received, but there was nothing she could do about it now. As Sahara got off the phone, Jen just hoped that she wouldn't be too late. If she managed to get to him before he hurt someone, there was no reason why he would have to be put down.

This was different from the Vamp in the hospital or the Were that had attacked her and left the scars on the back of her shoulder. Bobby was a friend. This was personal.

When she pulled up to the address Sahara had given her, she saw a woman standing on the front lawn, looking further up the street. Rather than stop and ask the woman, who she assumed was Bobby's wife, what had happened,

Jen stepped on the accelerator and headed in the direction she was looking.

Over the roar of her motor, Jen heard the unmistakable sound of screaming from up ahead. Swearing and praying that Bobby hadn't done something awful, she cranked the wheel and followed the screams.

What she found was even worse than she had expected. In the middle of the road, almost at the end of the next block, was a bus and a large group of people standing around the front of it, looking, pointing, and gawking. Jen slid to a stop and grabbed her black case as she sprinted towards the crowd, afraid of what she would find inside.

"Did it do that on purpose?" she heard one person comment as she pushed through the crowd.

"Yeah, it just ran into the bus, like it thought it was a charging bull or something."

"Is it dead?" One of them asked, and Jen fought back the urge to scream at them to just shut up.

Jen had never seen Bobby in full wolf form, her first sighting of him wasn't a pleasant one.

He was wedged almost completely inside the crumpled front end of the bus. As the gawkers had said, it truly looked as though he had run into the bus at full speed, likely while the bus was in motion. She was relieved to discover that he was still alive, evidenced by the growling and snarling that she could hear as she approached. "Bobby?" she said as she got close. "If you can hear me, it's Jen."

From the way his body was twisted, Jen had an easy time guessing that his back had been broken in the impact. As she moved closer, he growled louder and snapped at her, but she was too far out of his reach for him to connect.

She stopped where she was and opened her case. "My team's on the way," she said as she pulled out a pair of syringes. "These are a tranquilizer to calm you down and a painkiller. You're hurt and I think you know that." She stepped forward, being careful to stay as close to his feet as she could. Reaching out with one arm and keeping her body as far away from him as she could, she stabbed the needle into his haunch and depressed the plunger.

"I know you don't want to hurt anyone,"

she explained as she dropped the used syringe back into her case and opened the cap on the second, "and you won't. Just try to calm down."

In the distance, she could hear sirens approaching. Her phone rang but she couldn't take the time to answer it. She looked over at one of the onlookers who had gotten too close, a boy who appeared to be about fifteen or so, and called him towards her. "Could you answer my phone, please?" She turned her hip so that he could easily reach it before turning back to the howling Were.

As the crowd pressed in closer, his growling and howling had increased and Jen noticed that the tranquilizer wasn't working as quickly as she had hoped it would. At the end of one long, drawn-out howl, he turned his head away from the crowd and sank his razor-sharp teeth into the bus's tire, puncturing it with every fang.

"He says to tell you that they're almost here," the young man with Jen's phone called over to her. "And there are ambulances coming, too."

"Thanks," she responded without looking away from Bobby. She wasn't sure if giving him the painkiller would cause him to hurt himself further but she couldn't handle seeing him in that much pain. Against her better judgment, she plunged the second needle into his flank and injected him with the werewolf-strength morphine.

"Tell him that his back's probably broken but it doesn't look like he hurt anyone," she called over her shoulder.

As the boy relayed her message, Jen reached down into her case again for another tranquilizer. If she remembered correctly, a Were of Bobby's size could take five doses of the chemical before any chance of an overdose but Jen didn't feel comfortable giving him any more than one more after this one. "Tell him that he's had two tranqs and a pain, okay?" Without waiting for an answer, she injected the Were with the second dose of tranquilizer.

To her relief, Bobby started to relax and his howling ceased altogether. His teeth were still buried in the tire but his panicked eyes and the unceasing growls made sure that she knew he was far from unconscious.

What felt like hours later, she heard her team pushing their way through the crowd, shouting at people to make them back away. Marc dropped to a knee next to Jen and began attaching silver shackles to Bobby's hind feet. "Are you okay?" he asked, looking up at Jen.

"I'm fine. He's one of Sahara's regulars and I was in the store when she found out."

He nodded while attaching the second shackle to Bobby's other foot. "I was going to ask you about that too."

J.J. and Ty worked on making a path for the emergency crews, who were waiting for the Were to be secure before moving in to take him to the hospital. Mike had taken the dangerous end and was busily trying to attach a silver-lined muzzle to Bobby's snout.

As soon as Marc was finished with the hind legs, he moved to secure the front ones as well. By the time he was finished, Mike was done as well and the pair of them backed away to let the medics have room to work.

Jen backed off also, picking up her case and moving over to the closest sidewalk. She looked around the crowd and spotted the kid that had her phone, who was still holding it and watching the action. She snapped her case closed and walked over to retrieve it. "Thanks," she said as she approached. "You were a huge help."

"Is it going to make it?" he looked at her, his eyes huge.

"Looks like it," she answered as she slipped her phone out of his hand. Looking around the crowd again, she spotted the woman who had been standing in Bobby's front yard. With another word of thanks to the teenager, she jogged over to the woman.

"Are you Bobby's wife?" Jen asked as soon as she was close enough.

The woman nodded. "I'm Lucy." She looked away from the medical crews that were gathered around her husband and met Jen's eyes.

"I'm a friend of Sahara's," Jen supplied. "I was there when you called her."

"I didn't know who else to call," Lucy sobbed. "If I'd called the police, they just would have shot him." She turned her pleading eyes back to the scene of the accident, where Bobby had been placed on a gurney and was in the process of being loaded into one of the waiting ambulances. "Is he going to be okay?" she asked.

"I think so." Jen raised a hand to Marc, who

appeared to be searching for her. When he spotted the gesture, he jogged over in her direction. "This is Lucy," Jen explained. "Bobby's wife."

Marc looked between the women. "Do you need a ride to the hospital?" he asked. "Or are you a Were also?"

Lucy shook her head. "No, I'm human so I can't ride with him, I know." She looked up at Marc. "A ride would be great."

"I'll take her," Jen offered. "And I'll meet you guys back at the office, if that's okay."

"Sounds fine to me," Marc responded. "I'll see you then." With that, he turned and jogged towards the rest of the team.

Jen took Lucy by the arm and led her towards her Jeep. "Let's get you on your way, shall we?" She opened the passenger door and helped Lucy climb inside.

After dropping her case into the back seat, Jen drove them towards the hospital. "He's going to be fine," she tried to reassure Lucy. "They have some awesome doctors on staff right now, so I'm sure he'll be taken care of."

"I just don't understand what happened," Lucy sniffed as they slowly crept past the increasingly-large throng of gawkers. "I know he's been pretty stressed out lately but I hadn't realized it was this bad."

"What was going on to stress him out so much?" Jen shot a glance at the woman, wishing that there was more she could do to help.

"It's that jerk with all the conspiracies, I know it." Lucy wiped some of the tears off her face with the sleeve of her sweatshirt. "He went around telling everyone about how Bobby got caught outside a few moons ago. Once everyone found out about it, they started being absolutely awful to him." She sniffed again. "To both of us, but they were worse to him.

"I know he didn't want to hurt anyone," she continued. "When he started to lose control, it was the last thing he said. He wanted me to get away from him but I didn't understand what he meant."

"And then he popped," Jen finished. Lucy, silent now, just nodded.

With a sigh, Jen pulled up in front of the emergency loading and unloading area. "Do you want me to come in with you?" She asked as Lucy opened the door to climb out.

"No," she shook her head. "Thank you for bringing me here, though." She smiled weakly at Jen before closing the door. "And thank you for going after Bobby." She closed the door and quickly walked into the building.

Chapter 15

Jen spent the next few days with Sahara, helping her out in the shop and using her phone book to research prospective therapists. Sahara tried to help as much as she could with Jen's search but soon left that to her friend.

They did get frequent updates from Lucy about the progress that Bobby was making towards recovery. Because his back had been broken and because he had continued to thrash around despite the damage, the doctors had been forced to re-break a part of his spine so that it could set properly. "At least werewolves heal quickly," Lucy had said when they expressed concern over the process.

When Jen got home on the third afternoon, however, she was met at the door by Troy. The hybrid had a wide, cat-and-the-canary grin on his face. "Guess what I found," he said, holding up a piece of paper.

"Umm," Jen said as she tried to figure out what he was up to. "I'm going to guess that you have paper. Congratulations."

"No," his grin didn't even falter at her lousy attempt at humor. "It's an address and phone number."

"Wow," Jen said as she stepped around him and into the house. "I hadn't known you were looking for a girlfriend." She made a beeline for the kitchen, hoping that there was coffee waiting. As good as Sahara's tea was, there was only so much of it that Jen could handle. "Bonus points for getting an address, though. Most people just give out numbers these days."

Troy sputtered and followed her inside, closing the door on the way. "His name is Jeriah Valentine, his license is current, and as far as I can tell, he's still accepting patients. He has a home office and apparently walk-ins are acceptable."

As his words sank in and began to make sense, Jen whirled around and snatched the paper out of Troy's hand. "This is the shrink you were talking about." She examined the paper, and all of the necessary information was there. "Awesome!" she exclaimed as she hugged Troy. She checked her watch, poured the cup of coffee into one of her travel mugs, and headed for the door.

Dr. Valentine's office was located in his house, as Troy had said, but Jen was surprised when she pulled up in front of the large building. It was almost twice the size of hers, deep heather grey with darker accents and she figured that business must be good for him to afford a place like that. Hopefully that meant that he was a better therapist than the last two she had encountered. She parked on the street in front of the house and stepped up the walkway, which had been cleared of snow and salted to prevent ice from forming. Small lights placed every few feet along either side of the path to clearly light the way.

When she knocked on the front door, a small panel slid open and she saw a pair of dark-rimmed brown eyes peering out at her. "Can I help you?" the person asked.

"My name is Jen Rice, I was hoping to speak with Dr. Valentine," Jen explained.

The face behind the door nodded and the panel snapped shut. With barely any noise, the door swung open. "Come in," the same voice said, although its owner wasn't visible.

Curious and more than a little cautious, Jen stepped inside, where she found a pale-haired young woman standing behind the door. Jen could understand why she was hidden behind the doorway because it appeared that all she was wearing was a mile or so of burgundy colored lace.

The woman smiled at Jen and led her deeper into the house. The inside was much darker than the exterior had been and most of the rooms had the lights turned completely off. The wooden-floored hallway was the only brightly-lit area and Jen followed the woman along it until she stopped at the last door on the left.

The woman knocked twice on the door before cracking it open. "Miss Jen Rice is here to see you," she informed someone on the other side of the door before looking back at Jen once more. "Would you like a drink? Coffee or tea, perhaps?"

Never one to turn down free coffee and realizing that she had forgotten her travel mug out in the Jeep, Jen accepted her offer. "Coffee, please." She tried not to stare, as she had been trying while following the woman down the hall but the skimpy outfit left almost nothing to the imagination. Besides, Jen remembered that Troy had mentioned this doctor was active in the bondage community and she wasn't sure whether it would be ruder to look or not to.

With another smile, she pressed the door open further for Jen and backed away. "He's ready for you."

Jen looked at the door without being able to see anything inside for a long moment. She wasn't sure what she would find on the other side of the door and she hoped that whatever was there wouldn't be too bad. With a deep breath, she straightened her back and stepped into the room. She was here to find a therapist for her friends and she would do whatever she could to help them.

To her surprise, the office that she had

been shown to wasn't frightening at all. There was a large mahogany desk on one side of the room with a pair of thick, plush chrome and black leather couches and matching tables and lamps. A handful of degrees and certificates hung on the wall behind the wooden desk, which made Jen feel a little more secure in her decision to talk to this therapist. At least the guy had training, an improvement that she seriously believed the previous two therapists had lacked.

Behind the desk sat a man with long, wavy black hair, a deep blue collarless shirt that looked like it was made out of silk and black leather pants. He was barefoot, which she could see by the fact that his feet were perched on the edge of the table, crossed at the ankles.

Jen froze only a couple of steps into the room, no longer sure that this was a good idea. She swallowed hard as the man looked up from the medical chart he had been perusing and smiled at her. "Nice to meet you," he said as he dropped his feet to the floor, stood up, and walked around the desk to offer her a hand to shake. "How can I help you today?"

"I..." Jen stammered, "I have this friend." She swallowed again and shook his hand. "Actually, it's more like a group of friends."

He smiled down at her again and Jen realized that he was at least three inches taller than her. Although she had never seen a man wearing black leather pants before outside of the biker gangs in movies, he wore them well. "I know a lot of people who have those friends." He motioned towards a couch. "Have a seat."

Jen took another deep breath and stepped over to the offered couch while Dr. Valentine walked back over to his desk. "Why don't you tell me about your friends?"

Jen took another look around the room while she gathered her thoughts. "They were held for a long time, although some were there longer than others and they were all abused pretty badly." She looked back at him and folded her hands in her lap so that she wouldn't start to fidget. "I was told that you were kind of a specialist in certain..." she looked around the room again, "things."

He nodded slowly and his grin slowly faded.

"These friends of yours, was the abuse from their dominant partner or from someone else?"

Before she could answer, there was a tap on the door. The young woman who had shown Jen into the office walked into the room, carrying a tray with two cups of coffee, a bowl of sugar cubes, and a small pitcher of cream. She settled the tray onto the wooden desk after handing out the cups, smiled at each of them once more, and asked, "Do you need anything else?"

Dr. Valentine smiled at her. "No, thank you." He looked over at Jen to explain, "This is Amber, my assistant. As such, all privacy clauses apply to her as well."

Jen wasn't sure what he meant by that but was willing to accept it. She watched as Amber smiled at each of them again and left the room.

"It wasn't a partner, not really. They were prisoners and held for entertainment." She looked back up at him and explained about what life had been like in the demons' lair, without going into any real specifics.

"And are these friends of yours still there?"

Jen shook her head. "They've all been rescued

and treated medically but that's about it for now. They have a therapist that's assigned to them but he doesn't understand where they're coming from. The last time I went over to see them, some of them mentioned that they had been into, well, a certain lifestyle before being taken and that kind of changes the playing field."

He nodded slowly as she spoke, listening carefully. "And how do you fit into all of this?" He asked her once she was finished.

Jen debated on just telling him that it had been her team that had rescued the people but if he agreed to treat them, he would discover the truth anyway. Beyond that, she still needed someone to take her for five sessions of therapy before she could get David off her back. With a sigh, she looked up at him. "I was there with them for about a month before we were all rescued."

"And were you into this lifestyle before all of this happened?"

She shook her head. "No. I didn't even know there *was* something like that until they told me." She took a sip of her coffee before looking back up at him sheepishly. "To be honest, I really don't know anything about it, and it seems really strange to me."

"It's not for everyone," he admitted. "Some enjoy it and some don't. It's all about personal choice." He took a drink of his own coffee, evaluating her over the edge of his cup. "I get the feeling that there's more you aren't telling me."

"I'm mostly worried about them," Jen offered. "I just need five sessions so my boss doesn't get in trouble over it. But they don't have anyone with them who understands what they're going through and, like I said, their therapist just doesn't get it."

"I understand that," he said as he set his cup back onto the desk. "And I'm willing to help them if they need it as badly as you believe they do. However, you seem to be in a much different situation than they are in."

"It was my response team that came to get everyone, so I've got that support behind me. Plus, I get to carry a gun and that makes me feel a lot better, too."

He sighed and shook his head. "If carrying a weapon is what makes you feel safe, then I'm not going to try and tell you not to, especially if you're a response team member. However, since you said that you weren't familiar with this lifestyle before everything happened, then there's likely to be some additional trauma that you experienced differently than the rest of them did."

"Does that mean you're willing to see them?" Jen looked up at him hopefully. When he nodded and smiled at her, she broke into a grin. "Thank you, Dr. Valentine. I can't tell you how much I appreciate this."

"It's Jerry, please. And all I need to know is who I send the billing paperwork to."

She dug into a pocket and pulled out one of David's business cards. "It actually goes to Charlie Winters with the NPIB but I don't have his number. But that's my boss and he can get that for you."

Chapter 16

When she got home that night, Jen was surprised to discover that she had a visitor. A man
with short, light brown hair, rich brown eyes
and a friendly, close-lipped smile sat on her
couch. He was dressed in well-worn khakis and
a dark brown suede jacket. He stood to greet
Jen as she walked into the living room. "My
dear, it has been far too long."

"William, how've you been?" Although William was a vampire, Jen had absolutely no fear
of him. The pair had become friends a short
time ago, while Jen had been helping him search
for the Soul Gem that his daughter resided in.
"I see you aren't in prison."

Vanitha, the demoness who had stolen the
gem, had forced William to commit a series of

robberies in return for the safekeeping of his daughter. Desperate, William had committed the acts but after meeting Jen he had agreed to turn himself in and return the stolen items, once they were retrieved from the demoness.

The vampire chuckled. "No, the district attorney was surprisingly lenient, given the situation." He took Jen by both hands and kissed her on both cheeks. "And on that subject, I am here because I hadn't properly thanked you for your efforts in returning my darling Rachel to me." He pulled her over to the couch so that she could take a seat next to him. "And I am deeply saddened by what happened to you as a result of my request."

The demoness that had held Rachel was the same one that captured Jen and turned her over to Thaxter and Cylin. Although Jen had known that there were more people aware of what her situation had been, it still surprised her whenever someone mentioned it. "Don't worry about it," she waved his concern away. "It wasn't your fault. I'm just glad that you could get Rachel back." Although she hadn't been able to return Rachel to her father, Troy had taken William to Vanitha's house after she was arrested. The pair of them, along with Patrick, had searched the house to find Rachel's Gem and the rest of the stolen goods.

"So what have you been up to lately?" she asked him as he relaxed.

William sighed. "I've begun to research again, searching for a means of restoring Rachel to her previous life.

"How's that going?"

"Not well, I must admit. I haven't had much luck in finding a way to release her from her imprisonment. However," he looked up at Jen, hope shining in his eyes, "I've not given up. I am certain that a means will be discovered and I will simply do what I can to keep her safe until then."

Jen nodded her approval. "Sounds like a pretty good plan."

He smiled broadly at her, barely revealing a hint of his sharp fangs. "And until then, I have decided that I need to take better care of my-self as well. Rachel always complained that I didn't treat myself very well, so in honor of her, I have begun to develop better control over myself and my urges."

"Probably not a bad idea," Jen responded, not sure what he was getting at. "How are you doing that?"

"I've begun a new diet supplement that is designed specifically for vampires like me. It helps to relieve both the cravings and the rage-inspired impulses." He looked over at her, his grin fading as a more thoughtful expression replaced it. "I've heard of a lot of vampires who have been falling prey to their rage lately and the last thing I want is for something like that to happen to me. So if this supplement will help with my self-control, I will take it for as long as I need to."

"I hadn't heard of anything like that coming out on the market."

William chuckled again. "That's because you are not a vampire, my dear, and have no need to know of such things."

Jen had to admit that he had a point. After all, if it wasn't for her friendship with Sahara and the fact that she specialized in treatments for werewolves and hybrids, Jen would know next to nothing about those as well. "And this is working for you?"

"Yes, it is. I could feel the effects fairly quickly and every day it becomes easier to control my urges." As he spoke, his phone rang. He excused himself to answer it but then turned back to Jen. "I apologize," he said. "But that was my caseworker, reminding me that I am required to check in with him tonight. Please excuse me but I do hope that I will be allowed to come back and visit again soon."

"Of course," she agreed as she escorted him to the door. "You go do what you need to, and I'll talk with you again soon."

As she closed the door behind him, she couldn't help but feel a sense of unease, as though something was terribly wrong. She leaned her back against the door, trying to decide what it was but came up with nothing. "Maybe it's just because I'm tired," she told herself. Although she had gotten the herbal tea from Sahara a few days ago, she hadn't started to use it yet. With a sigh, she headed to the kitchen to boil some water. "I'll get some decent sleep tonight," she muttered.

As she headed upstairs with her cup of tea, however, she discovered that her nighttime plans would have to wait. When she opened her bedroom door, she discovered a man there, sitting on the carpet in front of her dresser and brazenly digging through her drawers.

"What the hell do you think you're doing?" she asked as she put her cup down on the nightstand and glared at him.

Thaxter looked up at her, holding up a sheer red negligee that he had apparently found buried in the drawer. "Put this on."

"No." She looked at the demon in astonishment, surprised both by his command and her refusal. "Put that back." Above and beyond the fact that she wasn't particularly partial to the lingerie, which had been a gift from an ex-boyfriend years before, she especially wasn't willing to just blindly do as she was told. Especially where the incubus was concerned.

He rose fluidly to his full height and stepped closer to her, towering over her and holding the scrap of satin and lace in one hand towards her. "I said to put it on, and you will do as you are told," he growled at her.

She snatched the clothing out of his hand, wadded it into a ball, and tossed it behind her, aiming for the trash can but doubting that it hit its mark. "Stop trying to intimidate me," she glared at him. "I have two heavily armed men just down the hall who would really love to show you firsthand what happened to Cylin."

"You think you can threaten me?" He laughed as he stepped forward, took her by both arms, and tossed her onto the bed. "What makes you think I would have any reason to be afraid of your friends?"

Jen rolled off the other side of the bed and backed against the wall. She could feel the reassuring bulk of her pistol, still securely wedged in the back of her pants. She didn't draw it quite yet but if Thaxter thought she was defenseless, he was going to be surprised. "Why are you even here?" she called over to him. "Don't you have someone else to annoy?"

In a blink of an eye, he was in front of her, his hands on her face, tilting her head to force her to look up at him. "What does it take to make you shut up?" he asked as he lowered his face to hers. Just before he made contact, he stopped with an expression of surprise.

"I said no," Jen said as she pressed the barrel of her gun deeper into the demon's side. "You need to back off. I mean it."

Slowly, he took a step backward, followed by another one. As she cautiously watched, he leaned down over her to pick something up from the floor. He scooped the wadded-up lingerie that she had thrown onto the carpet and held it in front of her. "Put it on." His eyes were cold as he spoke, and his voice was even colder. Jen felt a chill run down her spine, and she wondered what he would do if she denied him again. Slowly, she reached out and took the garment.

Keeping a tight grip on her pistol with one hand, she untangled it with the other and held it up in front of her so that he could see it and then offered it towards him. "You want to see it on," she said. "Then *you* put it on."

He stood motionless for a long moment, looking down at her, the gun, and the lingerie. "Must you be defiant even in this?" he asked quietly. "Is it this stubbornness of hers that caught their interest?" He mused, almost as though to himself.

"I have no idea," she answered. "I don't even know who *they* are."

He blinked slowly at her. "You understand me?"

"Of course I can..." Her voice trailed off as she realized, too late, that he wasn't speaking in any human language. With an oath, she pushed herself away from the wall.

"How long have you understood?" he asked, his eyes more curious than angry.

She shrugged. "A while, I guess." Without intending to, she had answered him in his own language and his eyes narrowed.

"How much do you know?" he demanded as he took a step closer to her.

The fuzzy feeling in her head, the one that had begun to feel all too familiar, started up again as he approached. She put a hand against his chest to stop him. "Don't do this; not right now."

"Do what?" he asked, but at least he stopped at the length of her arm.

"I can't think when you get too close," she admitted. "If you want to talk, then stay back."

He took a step away from her. "How can you know our language?" he asked as her breathing returned to normal. "Only very few humans have ever learned it."

"I don't know." When his eyes narrowed again, she replaced her gun in its holster, becoming more doubtful by the minute that he would try to hurt her. "I really don't. I just started to understand it while you and Cylin would talk to each other while we were still being held at your place."

"That explains how you came to know his name," Thaxter nodded. "I had wondered at that."

"And yours, and Vanitha's as well," Jen agreed. "Who are the Inquisitors?"

"They are nothing you need to worry about," Thaxter replied, a little too quickly for Jen to accept.

"But you said that you were protecting me from them," she pressed. "If that's the case, then I should at least know something."

The incubus's brows lowered again. "You

really are infuriating, do you realize that?" It looked as though he was about to step closer to her again but thought better of it. After glaring at her for a moment, he sighed and sat on the edge of her bed. "They are the monitors of my world, overseers who are responsible for ensuring that the Lords' edicts are followed."

"But how would they know about me?" Jen asked. "I hadn't ever been to your world before you brought me there."

The demon shrugged. "Occasionally they will be sent to your world, although it is rare. Usually it would only be to check on scouts who had been sent for the by the Lords to make sure that they are making progress toward their objectives."

She thought for a moment about all this. "There's a psychic who's been after me, the same one that you rescued me from. Is he one of these scouts?"

Thaxter shook his head. "No, he is human, although he wishes to become more." When she looked at him quizzically, he explained. "A human who is filled with enough energy from my world can undergo a ritual that will change him beyond what he is. If done correctly and by a powerful enough demon, that person could transform into a lesser demon himself."

"Become a demon?" Jen repeated. "I didn't know that was possible."

"It is," he agreed, "but it is very rare. Only a few know how to perform the rite of change and it is only ever used on those few humans who have performed some great service to us."

Jen sighed. "Somehow I doubt that just killing me would be considered that great of a service."

"You may be surprised by that," Thaxter disagreed. "I am unsure why, but the Inquisitors have taken a strong interest in you. When you were given to me, I was instructed to kill you immediately."

"So why didn't you?"

He shrugged. "At first, I thought you would make a nice plaything and perhaps provide enough entertainment to alleviate some of the boredom. But your steadfast refusal to accept me was surprising. I wanted to know how much it would take to get you to accept me."

"I remember you telling Cylin that he wasn't

pushing on me hard enough." She glared at the demon. "That pissed me off, you know."

Thaxter just shrugged it off. "After a while, Cylin started to notice that the energy he was taking from the humans had begun to diminish. When I came in to investigate, I noticed that you were drawing it away from us and into yourself.

"At first, it angered me because you had stolen what rightfully belonged to me. Then I came to realize that perhaps this power of yours could be used to my benefit. I wasn't sure how but I wanted to learn more. When I approached the Inquisitors about it, however, they weren't pleased with the idea. One of them was immediately angered that you yet lived but the rest of the group agreed to let me continue to work with you. As long as I controlled you, they also saw the benefit to having ability such as yours at our disposal."

"So I was just a... what?" she asked, "Some sort of a tool for you to figure out how to use?"

"Of course," he answered without blinking. "You are just a human, after all."

Jen felt something break inside of her at that

comment. She knew that she was just a human, not a mage or a psychic or anything special like that. Even so, she didn't like to have it thrown in her face that blatantly.

"Get out," she whispered, looking away from him. "Just leave."

She heard the bed squeak as he stood and for a moment, she was afraid that he was going to touch her again. Still, she refused to look in his direction. She could feel his presence, close enough to touch, but she fought the urge to reach out to him. *It's just his magic*, she told herself. Her fists tightened around the scrap of red fabric that she still clutched in her hands, squeezing tightly enough that she swore she was about to rip it. She didn't care. As long as she could maintain her dignity long enough for the incubus to leave, she would be okay.

After what felt like the entire lifespan of the universe passed, she felt his presence diminish. She couldn't hear him move but she knew as soon as he was gone. Still, she waited a long moment before looking over to where she knew he had been. Only empty space remained, there was nothing left to show that he had ever been there.

Fighting back tears, she stripped off her clothes and dropped them onto the floor. She slipped the pistol and its holster under her pillow, as had become her habit, and pulled back the covers of her bed. With a flip of the switch on the wall, her room was cast into darkness. As she pulled the covers up over her, the first tears dropped onto her pillow.

On the nightstand, cold and forgotten, her cup of tea sat.

Chapter 17

Late the next morning, Jen decided it was time to stop by and see how the group was doing. She figured that it'd be a good idea to let them know that she had found a new therapist for them and looked forward to seeing the look on Maureen's face when she did.

When she pulled up to her normal place on the street, she discovered that there was already another car parked there. A bright silver Audi, only a few years old, was parked in her spot. Growling, she pulled up behind it and shut off the ignition. Pulling her papers out of the glove box, she stepped out onto the curb and headed up to the house.

When she knocked at the door, Maureen opened it as usual. This time, however, she looked more irritated at Jen's presence than normal. "They're in therapy," she snarled at her. "Not that I expect you to care."

"Nope," she answered. "Not really." Without waiting for Maureen to open the door all the way, Jen stepped around her and ducked into the house.

She could hear the sound of voices coming from further in the building and followed them to the living room. Inside, she saw the entire remaining group but this time they weren't sitting on folding chairs that had been brought in for the session. Now, they were perched in their usual places on the couches, the recliner, and even sprawled out on the floor. In the middle of the group sat a man with long, dark hair.

As Jen looked for a place to sit and wait for their session to be over, Jerry looked up and noticed her. Smiling broadly, he waved her to come forward. "Join the party," he said as he grinned.

Cautiously, Jen stepped forward. "I hadn't meant to interrupt," she tried to explain. "I didn't realize you were here already."

"All things considered, I figured there wasn't

any point in waiting. As soon as I got authorization from Agent Winters, I decided to head on over."

No wonder Maureen was in such a bad mood, Jen realized. The woman obviously worshipped Dr. Lycheck and now he had been replaced without warning. On one hand, Jen could understand the caretaker's aggravation but on the other hand, she didn't care. Despite the warning glare that Maureen shot at her from across the room, or perhaps because of it, Jen walked into the group and sat in an open space on the couch.

As soon as she was seated, Bailey was at her feet. He sat on the floor in front of her, leaned against her legs and rested his head in her lap. Jen absently stroked his hair as she looked around the rest of the group.

Jon had apparently reclaimed his recliner but Andre hadn't given up the fight. The wiry young man perched on the back of the chair, just behind Jon, with his feet on the armrests and waiting for the larger man to move. Amy sat on the floor a few feet to the side of Jerry, watching him intently and absently twirling her hair. Anna sprawled on the other couch with Christy lying in front of her.

As Jen looked around the group, she noticed that Zack wasn't there. Before she had a chance to ask, however, she heard footsteps coming from the kitchen. Zack walked into the room, an enormous bowl of potato chips balanced in one hand and a pair of plastic dip containers in the other. A grin broke across his face as he saw Jen and he padded directly towards her.

He sat on the couch next to her and held the chips out toward Jen. "Want some?" he asked.

She scooped a handful of chips out of the bowl. "Thanks." As she took a bite, Zack put the bowl and both dip containers onto the table and scooped out a few chips for himself.

As the rest of the group descended on the munchies, Jen realized that Bailey was eyeing the chips but had made no move towards them. She pulled a chip out of her small pile and offered it to him.

Watching her carefully, he picked his head up and leaned towards the offered snack. He took the chip in his mouth and dropped back onto her lap. She continued smoothing his hair and feeding him chips while the rest of the group settled down.

"Okay, who haven't we heard from?" Jerry asked as soon as the room was quiet enough for him to be heard. "Anna, how are you doing today?"

"Okay, I guess," she shrugged. "It was hard when everyone left and I had to sleep by myself again but it's getting easier."

Jerry looked around the group. "Is anyone else having a hard time sleeping alone?"

A few people raised their hands but only Christy spoke up. "I have to leave the lights on," she admitted. "I can't sleep where it's dark." Everyone nodded their agreement.

"At first," Jon offered, "it was the opposite. I didn't like being out in the light but now I just don't like it to be dark."

"I have a flashlight I keep with me," Anna said. "I probably wake up ten times every night and look around the room with it before I can go back to sleep."

"So keeping a light with you helps?" Jerry asked. When she nodded, he looked around at everyone else. "Anybody else developing tricks to help them sleep at night?"

"I leave my bedroom light on," Jon explained. "That way, if I wake up in the middle of the night, I can see immediately that there's nothing there."

A couple of people had similar things that they did to help them sleep but then Jerry turned to Jen. "How about you? How are you sleeping?"

Jen blinked at him for a moment, finishing the chip she had in her mouth. "I have nightmares," she admitted, "but I have a friend that gave me some tea that has helped relieve them in the past."

"What about when you wake up? How do you deal with that?"

She thought for a moment. "Well," she answered, "I guess there are a few things that help with that. First of all, my brother and another friend are staying with me and it's reassuring to know that they're just down the hall. Besides that, I keep a gun next to my bed in a drawer."

She sighed before continuing. "I think that the biggest thing that helps me is that I know

Cylin's dead and he can't come back and hurt me anymore."

"It'd be a lot worse if he was still out there somewhere," Amy agreed.

Jen decided against mentioning that Thaxter was still roaming free. She didn't feel as though he was a threat to the rest of the group because, as far as she could tell, he hadn't made contact with any of them. Beyond that, she didn't want to scare any of them with the idea that he could. Almost as though he was reading her mind, Jerry looked at her directly as she thought, but she shook her head ever so slightly.

He took the hint and didn't press the issue. Instead, he discussed a handful of options with the group, tips on helping them to sleep better at night. Since some of them had decided to share beds, he didn't discourage the practice. "If that's what helps you," he explained, "I see no reason to change."

To Jen's relief, he didn't try to force anyone to speak if they didn't want to. He gave every-one a chance to say something if they wanted to speak but didn't press the issue if they remained silent. Even Bailey, who chose not to join the conversation, relaxed when he realized he wouldn't be in trouble and just watched the discussion from his position on Jen's lap.

"Okay everyone," Jerry said once he was finished. "Thanks for letting me have so much of your time but I think it's time I let you think over everything we talked about." He pushed himself up to his feet and smiled at everyone. "I'll be back in just a couple of days, so if any of you think of anything you want to discuss next time, let me know and we can cover those too."

"Actually," Jon spoke up. "If you have a minute, there's something I want to ask you about before you leave."

"Sure, what's that?" Jerry asked as he turned toward Jon.

"I know that Dr. Lycheck told us that we could go home if we felt like we were ready and that we'd be fine once we got there but a lot of us just don't have anywhere to go, which is why we're still here. However," he said as he shot a look over at Maureen, who still stood, scowling, by the door, "there are a lot of things here that just aren't working for us. So we were wondering what you thought about our moving out of here and getting one big place for all of us.

"We have a fund available to us, until we get our feet under us again, and a few of us have already started looking for jobs." He looked a little sheepish as he continued. "We can't just keep riding the system, eventually we need to start trying to have normal lives again."

Jerry looked thoughtful at the idea. "Are all of you in agreement that this is something you want to do?" he asked as he looked around the group.

Almost everyone nodded. "We've already been split up once," Christy spoke up, "and none of us are ready to separate any more than we have to but we've got to get out of here."

"That's ridiculous!" Maureen interrupted. "You people are here so that you can have someone keep an eye on you and take care of you, there's no reason to go off and do something stupid like that."

She would have said more, but Jerry interrupted her. "We appreciate your concern," he said, "but it's their decision to make, not yours."

Maureen sputtered at his statement. "If you

think they're ready to move out on their own, you're even more of a fool than I thought you were." She pointed over at Zack, who was busily scooping the last of the dip out of one of the containers. "That one won't even put clothes on and you think he's ready to be out on his own?"

"He wouldn't *be* out on his own," Jon whirled on her. "He'd be with us, where he belongs."

"And you think you know where he belongs?" she scoffed. "What makes you the expert all of a sudden?"

"Ten years of being his best friend, that's what," Jon answered, his voice rising in anger. "Just because you don't give a damn about us doesn't mean we don't give a damn about each other."

Jerry stepped in between them as the pair continued to bicker. "Calm down," he said quietly. "There's no reason for us to be yelling.

"I can see your point," he told Jon, "and I agree that if you guys feel that you are ready to move out, that you should be allowed to. However," he said as he looked over at Maureen, "she has a point. Until Zack is willing to wear clothing, it's going to be difficult for you guys to find a place."

Jon looked over at Zack. "Is it really worth it to you to stay here?" he asked, his voice much quieter this time.

Zack simply shrugged. "I tried; you know that."

"I have an idea," Andre piped up. He looked over at Jen. "Do you think there's any way you could take him for a few days until we got into our new place?" He looked from Jen to Jerry, and then over at Jon. "That way, all we have to do is bundle him up and take him from one place to the next, he won't even have to meet the landlords."

"No," Jon said before Jen could answer. "She's already done enough for us; we can't ask her to do that."

Jen thought while they debated the issue. While she wouldn't have any problem having Zack come and stay with her for a few days, she wasn't really sure where she would put him, or how Patrick and Troy would react to having him there. As she thought, she realized there was a much larger issue. "Jerry?" she said, "could I ask you about something in private?"

"Of course," he answered.

Jen detached herself from Bailey and stood up. She walked toward the kitchen, where hopefully she and Jerry would have a bit more privacy. Once they were inside, she looked over at him and sighed. "I don't have a problem letting Zack come and stay with me," she explained.

"I got the feeling that you wouldn't. But I also get the idea that there's something the rest of the group doesn't know."

She sank into one of the chairs that sat around the kitchen table. "The other demon, Thaxter, is still around," she explained. "I don't think he's a threat but I don't know how badly Zack would react if he saw him."

Jerry's eyes widened in surprise at her admission. "Why don't you think he's a threat?" he asked carefully.

"I don't know," she said. "But as far as I know, he hasn't tried to make contact with anyone here; he hasn't even mentioned them except in passing. But he hasn't tried to hurt me at all and I've been waiting." She snickered. "He didn't even try to hurt me when I had my gun pressed to him and I think that if he was going to do anything, he would have done it then."

"And you've seen him more than once?" When Jen agreed, he sighed. "How about you tell me about it from the beginning? That way I'll have a better idea of where you're coming from."

After taking a deep calming breath, Jen explained about everything that had happened between herself and Thaxter since her return home. She told him about how the demon had saved her from the psychic and how he seemed to still believe that she belonged to him. She described their conversation about the Inquisitors, and had to wipe a tear away as she spoke. "He drives me crazy," she pointed out, "and he's absolutely infuriating but I really don't think he'd hurt me."

Jerry slowly nodded as she finished the story. "Yet you're on relatively good terms with him for now, so long as it's at a distance."

"I know it's just because of his magic, he's an incubus after all, but even when he's not in my head, any time he gets too close to me, I can't think about anything but him."

"I think I know what's happening," he said, "but I'm not sure how much you're going to like it."

She blinked at him in surprise. "You do? What is it?"

"First of all, if everything you're saying is true and not just a really complicated deception on his part, I have to agree with you that you probably aren't in any danger. I can't say for certain but for now I'd be willing to take that chance."

Jen let out a breath that she hadn't been aware she had been holding. "That's good to hear." Even though she had been reasonably sure that her interpretation was right, it was nice to have another person agree with her. "So what do you think it is?"

He took a seat across the table from her and crossed his hands in front of him. "Why did you get so upset when he left the last time?" he asked.

Jen blinked at him in confusion, and then

thought about it. "He said something," she answered quietly. "Something that bothered me."

"Was it a threat?" When she shook her head, he asked, "What was it?"

"That I was just a human," she answered. "I know it's stupid, but it hurt."

"Why?"

"I don't know," she said. "Because it's true? I mean, he's a demon, so of course he'd see things that way."

"And you know what he is, right?" She nodded again, confused. "So why did it upset you so much?"

"Because I don't like the idea of just being someone's toy," she finally admitted. "I know it's stupid, but he'd been acting like I was something important but then all of a sudden that was gone." She felt the tears welling up again as she spoke and quickly wiped them away before they could fall.

"And I would imagine that having a conversation with a demon is difficult," he said. "Are you afraid of him still?"

"Not really," she disagreed. "The biggest problem is that he had this... I guess an aura effect that surrounds him. It makes my brain all fuzzy when he turns it on. But as long as he's not too close to me, we can talk just fine."

"Did you tell him that what he said hurt you?"

Jen shook her head. "I just told him to leave."

"And he did? That's surprising." When she looked at him with questioning eyes, he explained. "If he's just playing with you, why would he have left? Wouldn't he stay around to continue the game?"

She thought for a long moment before answering. "He stayed for about a minute, I could feel him there but he didn't say anything."

"And why do you think he did that?"

She shrugged. "Maybe he didn't understand what he did." She looked up at him. "He *is* a demon, after all."

Jerry smiled at her. "I think that if you can talk to Thaxter and see if he would be willing to leave Zack alone while he's at your house, things should work out all right. I believe that as long as you explain that you aren't rejecting him, just wanting to keep your friends from getting hurt, he'll react better to that.

"What about the other one? Did you react this way to him too?"

Jen shook her head emphatically. "No. I hated him, every time he took me out into the torture room. I still hate him, even knowing that he's dead."

Jerry leaned back in his chair. "Bailey reacts really well to you, I'm sure you've noticed. As soon as you enter the room, he runs over to you, almost as though you're his whole world."

"I don't know why he does that, he did it the first time I came over here and every time I've been over since."

"For whatever reason, he feels a really strong connection to you. Zack seems to feel it too but he doesn't show it as much as Bailey does. He smiles more, he talks more, and he just seems to be a lot more relaxed when you're around."

"Really? I hadn't noticed that."

"I think that's part of the reason that Andre suggested you take him in. Most of the rest of the group has seen what I see, or at least I think they have. However, I have some concerns about you taking Zack in."

"I thought you said it'd be fine as long as I talked to Thaxter beforehand."

"Yes, and I still believe that. However, I think that Bailey might view it as a rejection."

Jen blinked over at him. "I don't understand."

"When it comes to submissives, especially ones who have been hurt, it's important for them to find a new dominant partner that they can trust. In cases like those, it's frequently the sub who selects their partner and not the other way around."

"And you think Bailey's selected me?"

"From where I stand, it's fairly obvious. He isn't very forthcoming with his wishes very much but he's been quite forward on his opinion of you."

"So I'd have to take Bailey in too, or else that'd hurt him more?"

"In my opinion, yes. However, if you are completely against the idea, I can work with him to try and redirect his attention elsewhere."

"But," she looked around the room as she thought. "I don't know how to do any of that stuff. I don't think I *could* do any of that suff."

He shook his head. "You don't have to do

anything. All he needs right now is for someone to show him that they care about him, that he's more than just an object. He needs the emotional far more than he needs the physical."

Jen nodded, almost without thinking. "As long as you're sure it'll help them. I'm just worried that I'll do something to hurt one of them without meaning to."

"Well, we still have some time before anything has to be decided but I think it'd be a good idea if we sat down with the pair of them to discuss it more. That way, everyone knows what's going on, so there shouldn't be too many surprises."

"Sounds like an idea," she agreed. "Besides, I still need to talk it over with Patrick and Troy to let them know what's going on, too."

Jerry looked at her curiously. "Anyone I need to be worried about?"

"Nope," she shook her head. "Patrick's my brother and Troy's a friend that consults for New World. Both of them were part of the rescue team."

"So they both know what happened, that'll help, too." He stood and offered her a hand up as well. "But we should get back out to check on them before Maureen does any more damage."

Jen had to chuckle at that as she followed him out into the living room.

Chapter 18

After she left the group home, feeling a lot better, Jen decided that it was past time to stop in to check on her parents. She still felt bad about how their last dinner date had gotten mangled, so she wanted to make the effort to fix things, if she could. As she turned towards their hotel, she wondered if her mother had calmed down yet. The last time Jen had spoken to her over the phone, Janice had still been screeching about how she hated Jen's job and couldn't understand why she had gone out after a vampire on her own like that. She wasn't sure how Janice would react to what had happened to Bobby.

The streets were surprisingly clear, considering there were only a few days left before Yule.

Generally, traffic would be at its heaviest right then as last-minute shoppers brawled over the latest craze in children's toys that their kids absolutely had to have under the Yule tree and the most persistent of procrastinators realized that they were about to become divorced if they didn't manage to produce something.

She parked and headed upstairs. When she knocked on the door of their hotel room, Dean answered, a smile immediately spreading across his face. "Well, isn't this a surprise," he said as he ushered her inside. "Janice, look who's here."

Janice looked up from the magazine she was reading. "I was wondering how long it would take before you dropped in." She looked pointedly at her watch. "Is this your way of saying that we are welcome to come over to celebrate Yule?"

"Of course you are," Jen answered as she gave her mother a hug. "I've just been pretty busy lately, that's all."

"That job of yours, no doubt," Janice said. "Why won't you even consider getting a safer position somewhere else?"

"Do we have to argue about this again right now?"

"That's right," Dean agreed. "After all, it's almost the holidays, so we should be celebrating and being happy, not fussing and arguing over everything."

"Well, at least you don't look like you're hurt," Janice said grudgingly. "After what happened at the restaurant, I was expecting you to look much worse."

"Nope, I'm okay. But speaking of the restaurant, had you found another place for us to have the pre-Yule dinner?"

Janice shook her head. "Everything's booked solid until after Yule's already over. Even looking for a table for just five of us was impossible."

"Five?"

"Of course. Your father and I, you and Patrick, and we couldn't leave poor Troy at home all alone. It's the holidays, after all."

Jen almost winced at the idea. Her mother was apparently still trying to play matchmaker and had set her sights firmly on Troy.

"Speaking of which," Janice continued. "I still don't understand why everyone else isn't out here already. I know that Todd said he was working on getting caught up at work but there's no reason that everyone can't be together now."

"Actually, that's my fault too," Jen admitted. "I got into a bit of trouble not too long ago and everyone came out to help me with it."

"What happened?" Dean asked, and Janice leaned forward as well to hear the details, but Jen waved them off.

"We don't need to get into all that right now. Everything's fine, so there's nothing to worry about." She looked between her parents, who obviously weren't pleased at her dismissal. "How about Carter's? They've got really good food and we won't even have to worry about reservations."

"We haven't been there before, have we?" Dean looked over at his wife, who shook her head. "Okay, it sounds like an idea." He picked up his jacket from where it had been tossed on the back of a chair. "We were trying to decide where to go anyway."

Janice grudgingly stepped into her shoes and picked up her purse and coat. As she headed for the door, she pulled out her phone. "Does your brother know where this place is?" she asked Jen as she dialed.

"He was the one who told me about it."

Since she knew the way, Janice and Dean rode with Jen to the restaurant. Carter's was a warm, comfortable restaurant, not as snooty and expensive as most of the places that Janice normally dragged them to but quite a bit classier than Taco King.

As they walked in and were shown to a table, Jen groaned. With everything else that had been going on, she had almost forgotten about the NPIB agents who had been hounding her. Now she was face to face with them, as they were only a couple of tables away from where she and her parents were directed. While Janice and Dean took their seats, the agents sauntered over towards them.

"Miss Rice," Agent Thompson said once they were close enough to be heard without having to raise his voice. "We were just starting to wonder what had happened to you." His smile, though not cruel, was nowhere near pleasant.

"You haven't been home very much," Agent

Brooks chimed in. His eyes flashed over the other people at Jen's table dismissively. "We thought something had happened to you again."

Jen stopped before taking her own seat. She turned to face the agents, less than amused at their interruption. "Do we really have to do this now?" she asked, careful to keep her voice low. "I'm trying to have dinner with my parents." She tried not to grit her teeth as she spoke, galled at having to act so politely but she knew her mother would have a fit if she started yelling and throwing things at people while they were still in the restaurant.

Both of the agents looked down at Dean and Janice with interest. "Well now," Agent Thompson muttered. "Isn't that interesting?"

"Could we at least take this outside?" Jen asked before either of them had a chance to say something stupid.

"Of course not," Janice said as she looked up from the wine menu. "We've only just arrived after all, so there's no reason for them to chase you outside already."

Jen looked down at her mother in surprise,

not sure what she was up to. The agents, on the other hand, snickered.

Janice coolly glanced up from her menu to appraise both men. "Friends of yours, I assume?" When both of them only blinked in response and Jen explained who they were, she set the menu down onto the table again. "I assume you have some form of identification?"

As the agents fumbled in their pockets and withdrew their badges, Janice took a sip of the complimentary water their server had deposited onto their table. Once she had both their badges in hand, she opened her purse, pulled out a small notebook and tiny silver pen, and began writing down every piece of information that was in their identifications.

As the agents sputtered, Janice glanced up at them again. "I'll also need to know your supervisor's name."

"We're not required to give you that information," Agent Brooks protested.

"No matter," she replied as she handed their badges back. "No matter how far down the line you are, both of you ultimately answer to Director Bradford."

The agents blinked at her in surprise. "You're not trying to say that you know the director, are you?" Agent Thompson snickered.

"Of course," Janice answered as she tucked the notebook and pen back into her purse and took another sip of her water. "Who do you think organizes most of his community events?"

As the agents blinked at her in surprise, she calmly picked up her menu and went back to perusing it, her silent dismissal of the agents coming across loud and clear.

As the pair of men scurried back to their own table, Jen looked at her mother incredulously. "Do you really know the director of the NPIB?"

"Of course not," she replied. "But they don't have to know that. One of your father's companies takes care of a lot of the Board's outreach programs, so even if they do decide to run a search, they won't discover it.

"Besides," she said as she set her menu down. "I dislike it when my meals are interrupted, especially when it's for the second time."

Quietly laughing, Jen picked up her own

menu. She had almost forgotten how intimidat-
ing her mother could be when she was annoyed
and the meeting with the agents had served as
a quick but dangerous reminder.

Chapter 19

Jen, Patrick and Troy had managed to get all of the Yule decorations up, barely in time for the family get-together at her house. Although she recognized that she needed to get some more, Jen hadn't managed to find the time to go shopping for anything by the time Yule arrived and she knew that there wasn't any point in heading out then.

Above and beyond that, Jen decided that it was better that she hadn't gone out to find more decorations, as after Yule was over, everything went on sale, which was when she normally did the majority of her shopping anyway. Patrick and Troy, on the other hand, had waited a bit too long to start their Yule shopping and had run out of the house bright and early that morning in search of whatever may be left over.

Chuckling quietly, Jen poured herself another cup of coffee and headed upstairs, determined that she would get her shower and start getting ready early so that she wasn't caught unprepared as she usually was.

She stripped off her clothes as she walked across her room towards the bathroom, humming a holiday carol as she went and looking forward to a long, hot soak without any interruptions. In the bathroom, she turned on the hot water and checked to make sure that she had remembered to put her towel back on the rack before reaching into the shower to adjust the temperature. With a sigh of pleasure, she stepped under the spray and closed her eyes, enjoying the hot water on her chilled skin.

As she reached for the bottle of shampoo, she felt a familiar presence behind her. Without looking, she dropped her hand back down to her side and asked, "What do you want now?"

"You, of course."

She turned around to face him and almost stepped directly into Thaxter's lean, muscular chest. A few droplets of water had landed on the smooth surface. "Why are you here?"

"As I told you once before," he answered as he lowered his face toward hers, "you belong to me."

Jen shook her head slowly. "No, I don't." She looked up to meet his eyes, fighting to maintain control of her own mind. "But I would ask something of you."

"What?" he blinked at her in confusion.

She explained how she had agreed to let a couple of the guys stay at her house while the rest looked for a new place to live. "They don't know you're still around," she explained. "So you have to leave them alone."

He bit gently on the tip of her ear as he thought. "And if I grant you this indulgence, you'll agree that you are mine?"

When she only shook her head in response, he leaned back against the tiling that surrounded her shower, water from the overhead spray tracing rivulets down his body. "These friends of yours weren't mine anyway," he finally conceded. "They were Vanitha's. I have no use for them."

By the time Jen made it back out of the shower and got dressed, having finally convinced the incubus to let her bathe in peace, Troy and Patrick had already returned from their shopping spree. The men were in the living room, arguing over who got the last cookie from the package they had brought home with them. While they bickered, Jen calmly pulled the offending cookie out of the package and took a bite on her way into the kitchen in search of coffee.

"Hey!" they called after her once they discovered what she had done.

"What?" she called over as she turned the CD of Yuletide carols on and cranked up the volume. "I can't hear you!"

She pulled the punchbowl from the cupboard and started mixing the ingredients for the Yule punch, the only part of the meal that she was allowed to help make. While she mixed everything together, Troy checked on the enormous bird that had been roasting in the oven for most of the day and Patrick stirred the assortment of pots and pans that were scattered across the stove, some on the burners and some not.

Jen carried the punch out to set it on the dining table so that it would be ready when her parents arrived. As she hung the matching cups on their hooks along the edge of the bowl, she checked her watch and noticed that they would be arriving in less than a half hour. She pushed her still-damp hair out of her face and checked the living room again, partly to make sure that neither of the guys had been sneaking peeks at their presents but also to be sure that there weren't any weapons or other contraband in sight. The last thing she wanted was to give Janice a reason to start in on her.

Once she was sure that the living room would pass inspection, she darted out to the front lawn to be sure that the fire disc was ready to light. The blue cover that she had dropped across it earlier to keep the snow out was still in place, so she peeked under the cover to make sure there was wood inside it. She smiled as she discovered that not only had the guys stocked it as they had said they would but she could see the back of Patrick's truck sagging slightly under the weight of the extra wood he had brought home to keep it going.

Across the street, she saw one of her neighbors coming out to check on his own fire disc. He waved at her when he spotted her. "Got everything ready for tonight?" he called over.

She pointed towards Patrick's truck. "They brought extra just in case."

"Sure, but do you have starter fluid?" he laughed.

Up and down both sides of the street, she could see that most of her neighbors were ready to light their fires as well. While she was younger, being allowed to stay up late enough to come out and watch the fires being lit had been one of her favorite things about Yule and even as an adult it still brought a shiver of anticipation.

Back inside, she helped the guys move all of the food from the stove, oven, counters, and fridge over to the table. Once everything was in place, she lit all five of the candles that she had bought specifically for that night and went to do the same for the candles that lined the front windowsill. As she plugged in the million or so miles of small twinkling lights that she had strung both inside and outside the house, she grinned. She may not have had enough decorations but Yule lights were one thing that she was virtually guaranteed never to run short of.

As the sun settled down over the horizon and the shadows started to lengthen, more houses turned on their lights as well and soon it was almost as bright outside as high noon. Right on time, a sleek black sedan turned onto the block and parked behind Troy's car. Jen ran to the door to let her parents inside and everyone exchanged hugs before heading over to the heavily-laden table.

They laughed and talked as they ate, sharing stories of Yuletides past and singing along with the music when it suited them. Everyone got a good laugh out of Troy as he sang along with one of the carols, deliberately getting half of the words wrong. Any other day and that might have been annoying but there wasn't much that could bring the mood down on Yule.

By the time everyone had eaten their fill, it was almost completely dark outside. Without anyone having to say anything, they all got up as a group and headed outside. In the yard, Jen pulled the cover off the fire disc and stepped back. Since it was traditionally the man of the house who lit the fire, there were a couple of brief looks between Jen, Patrick and Troy over who would light it. After only a moment, however, Jen stepped back to let them figure it out on their own. It may have been her house but they were the closest thing to men she had living there.

Finally it was decided that both of them would light the fire, so they each took a small twig and lit it, standing on either side of the disc so they could light both sides at the same time. Jen grinned as the logs blazed, sending red embers shooting up into the air like fireworks. Up and down the street, more families were lighting their fires as well and soon there were small, bright patches of light as far as she could see.

As soon as the fire was going and didn't need anyone hovering over it to make sure it stayed lit, the group of them stepped into the street. Everyone else on the block was doing the same thing, wandering up and down the block in both directions and shaking hands and hugging everyone they met.

They stayed out until fairly late at night, exchanging end-of-year greetings with the neighbors and keeping their fire burning high. When everyone was too cold to stay outside any longer, they retired back into the house to get more food and dip into the punch, which now tasted suspiciously of rum. Dean looked over at Jen suspiciously as he tasted his but she smiled sweetly and shrugged her shoulders.

"Wasn't me," Troy insisted as he pulled out his own flask and took a nip.

"Should we open presents now?" Jen suggested as she stepped toward the living room. Everyone agreed that it was a good idea, so they followed her, drinks in hand, to exchange gifts.

Jen had to admit that Troy's gifts had been the most amusing. Apparently while he had been out with Patrick, the hybrid hadn't decided on a suitable gift for Dean and Janice. Instead, he handed over a card that was addressed to both of them. "I didn't know what kinds of things you guys liked, so think of this as a sampler platter."

When Dean opened the card, they discovered that the reason it was so thick was due to the dozen or so ten-dollar gift cards that were layered inside the card. There were cards for dinner out at a couple of restaurants, movie rentals, fast-food places, and even a home improvement store.

"I figured it this way," Troy explained as Dean and Janice dug through the stack. "You can stop for coffee, get something to eat for breakfast while you're out, and I'm sure there's something that needs to be fixed around the house; there always is."

As Janice chuckled, Troy continued. "Then once everything's done, you two can go enjoy a nice dinner out and then relax with a movie."

As everyone got a hearty laugh over his gift, there was a knock on the front door. J.J. poked his head inside to look around. "Hey!" he called out. "It's cold out here."

"Come on in," Jen said as she bounced up to give him a hug. "Happy Yule!"

"Happy Yule to you too," he said as he returned her hug and stepped aside so that the rest of the team could come inside too.

"We're making our rounds, so we figured we'd stop in and see you, too." Marc explained as he gave her a hug as well.

"Why didn't you say something?" Jen asked as she brought them into the living room. "I'd figured you were all doing family stuff."

He shrugged. "You said you had family coming over and we didn't want to interrupt that."

"But why aren't you guys with your families?"

"The kids are with their mother this year," Ty explained, "so I didn't have a whole lot of plans anyways."

Mike agreed. "My folks live out on the east coast, so I wasn't going to make them come all the way out here in the middle of winter. Besides, my dad doesn't travel well."

"So we just decided to do our own thing for the holidays," J.J. explained as he handed Jen a small colorful box. "That's from all of us."

She grinned and ripped the box open. Inside, there was a black short-sleeved shirt with a bright orange target printed on the front. On the back, the word "BAIT" was printed in large, bold letters. Laughing, she swatted Ty, who happened to be standing the closest to her.

"You guys are terrible," she snickered. "I have presents for you guys too but you have to wait until tomorrow to get them. I haven't wrapped them yet."

"Jen," Janice interrupted. "Aren't you going to introduce your friends?"

She looked up, startled. "Sorry, I completely forgot." She introduced each of her teammates to her parents, both of whom stood and shook hands with each of them as they were introduced. Jen couldn't help but notice Janice's appraising eyes travelling over each of the men as they were identified.

The guys stayed for a while, laughing and chatting with the family and partaking of the potent punch. Ty and J.J. parked themselves close to the table, doing their part to reduce the quantity of leftovers. Mike caught Troy taking another sip from his flask and demanded he hand it over so that he could try some also. When he took a drink, however, he gasped and sputtered. "What do you have in that thing, diesel?"

"So, you guys are all on the same team as Jen, is that right?" Dean cornered Marc. When

Marc nodded, he asked, "So what's it like? Is it all chasing down vampires in the middle of the night, or do you deal with other things too?"

"No, we do a lot of other stuff. Some of us are trained in Weres, poltergeists and other stuff too."

"And you have Jen help take these things out?"

Marc shook his head. "Jen's only certified for class one Weres and Vamps, so she's only allowed to go after the least dangerous of those."

Dean took another drink of his punch. "And what about the other things, poltergeists and whatnot?"

"Well," Marc thought for a moment. "I'm the only one that's class three certified in anything and the rest of the group's only class two. Once things calm down a bit more, maybe in a few months, we can work on getting Jen ready to test for her spirit qualifications too."

"Sounds pretty dangerous."

Marc had to laugh at that. "New World's still a pretty small company, so we don't usually get called out for the biggest things out there. When it comes to the big nasty beasties, we're pretty close to the last people who would be called over it.

"However, what we specialize in is containment; getting to problems and calming down the situation before it gets out of hand."

"That doesn't sound too bad at all," Dean nodded his agreement. "I have to admit, we were pretty worried when we found out that our Jen had started working with a response team."

"No problem," Marc said. "I'm sure most parents feel that way when they find out one of us has joined a team." He took another drink of his punch and added, "I know my parents weren't too happy about it either."

Janice, meanwhile, had moved closer to where Ty and J.J. were camped out at the table. "So," she said as she drained her cup of punch and handed the empty cup to Ty so that he could refill it for her. "Are either of you boys single?"

Chapter 20

When her phone rang a few days after Yule, Jen didn't think much of it, despite the fact that she didn't recognize the number. "This is Jen."

"Hey, this is Jon. How are you?"

"Doing pretty good, I guess. I was just going to stop by later and see how you guys were doing." She poured herself another cup of coffee and had a seat at the kitchen table. "What's up?"

"I got a job," he explained, pride in his voice. "There's a small mechanic shop not too far outside of downtown that's been looking for someone that can turn a wrench."

"I didn't know you were a mechanic."

"I'm not, at least not really. But they're willing to let me learn while I'm there so that I can get better.

"But that actually leads me to what I was really calling about," he explained. "Are you still willing to let Zack and Bailey stay there for a little while?"

"Of course," she answered. She had already talked it over with her roommates and Patrick had offered to let the boys have his room, since he wasn't going to be there for much longer anyway. "When do you need me to come pick them up?"

"Actually, Jerry offered to drive them. He said something about wanting to make sure that they adjusted to the new place."

She nodded, even though he couldn't see it. "That makes sense," she agreed. "So when are they going to be here? I want to make sure that if I have to be somewhere that someone will still be home."

"How's tomorrow afternoon? About three-ish?"

"I can be here for that, no problem."

When she hung up the phone, she went in search of her brother. He was lounged on the couch in the living room, watching some trivia game show and shouting the answers out to the TV. When he saw her walk into the room, he moved his feet so that she wouldn't sit on them.

"Are you still willing to let the guys use your room?" she asked.

"Yeah, no problem," he reassured her. "I've got the couch, so I'm not worried." He looked over at her and grinned. "So when are they coming?"

"Tomorrow."

"I guess that means I should go get my stuff picked up then, huh?" When she still looked uncertain, he reached over and squeezed her shoulder. "It'll be fine," he said. "And really, I don't mind."

"You sure?" When he nodded, she relaxed. "Okay. But I still feel like I'm throwing you out or something."

He laughed at that. "I've only got a couple of weeks left, and then I'm being sent out to the next build. So this actually makes it easier for me. It makes me get my crap together so I don't have to do the last-minute scramble to make sure I've got everything." He grinned down at her again as he stood up and stretched. "I don't know how many times I've had to call back to a place I just left to see if they can ship me something I forgot to pack."

"I just want you to know," she called after him as he headed for the stairs, "if you leave anything behind here, I'm holding it hostage until you come back for it."

As he disappeared up the stairs, she sighed and fell back against the couch cushions. She still felt bad about displacing Patrick that way but there wasn't really anywhere else to put the guys. "Besides," she reminded herself, "he offered, after all."

She was waiting anxiously at the window the next afternoon when the silver car came pulling up to park in front of her house. As soon as they stopped, she went over to the front door, holding it open for the group to come inside. Zack was the first to step out of the car, barefoot and dressed in an ankle-length overcoat. Jon stepped out behind him and pulled a medium-sized suitcase out with him. He set the case onto the sidewalk and waved at Jen as he helped Bailey out of the rear passenger seat.

Bailey was bundled up like a snowman,

dressed in a thick white snowsuit and gloves and boots to match. He loped across the yard towards Jen as soon as he was free from the car, his knees barely brushing the snow that still covered the ground and the small ball of bright blue fabric on the top of his beanie cap bouncing wildly as he ran.

Jerry followed them across the yard and grinned broadly as she was all but trampled beneath the sea of people who piled onto her. "Looks like you've got yourself a fan club there," he called over to her. Unable to say much, she just grinned at him in response.

Troy stepped around the pile of people and picked up the suitcase, which was only barely still clenched in Jon's hand. "I'll take this," he said as he hefted the case into the house. "It's going in Patrick's room, right?"

Jen nodded over at him. "My brother offered to let them use his room," she explained to Jerry as he raised an eyebrow.

"That was generous of him," he said. "Come on, let's at least get inside before you guys maul her." He reached down and pulled Zack off of

Jen so that they could step through the doorway and into the house.

As soon as they were inside the house, Zack stripped off the coat, revealing that he wasn't wearing anything underneath. When he tried to offer it back to Jerry, however, the therapist refused.

"You keep it," he said, "just in case you need it again later."

Bailey had a bit more difficulty getting out of his snow gear but between Zack and Jon helping, he was soon freed of it as well. Once everyone was comfortable, Zack, Jon and Bailey looked around the house in interest. Jon whistled low as he peeked further into the house. "Nice place you've got here," he said.

When Troy came back downstairs, everyone turned to look at him. He stopped three stairs from the bottom, waiting to see what the problem was.

"This is Troy, my roommate" Jen introduced him. "He was part of the team that came to get us."

"So he works with you?" Jon asked.

"I'm not a regular part of the team," Troy explained. "I'm a consultant and I've been known to step in to help out on occasion."

The guys visibly relaxed at that, and Zack took a step closer to Jen. "Can we have a look around?"

"Of course," she replied. "Make yourselves at home." Before she finished speaking, he and Jon were headed off to explore. Bailey, on the other hand, stayed close to Jen's side.

"If you aren't too busy, I'd like to talk with you for a few minutes," Jerry looked over at Jen and then at Troy as well.

"Sure," Jen agreed. "Coffee?"

"Sounds great."

Once she managed to detach her legs from Bailey's arms, Jen sent him off to explore also. "Go ahead, have a look around," she encouraged him. He didn't look overly thrilled at the idea of leaving her alone, but he obediently let go and headed off to catch up with the other two. Once he was gone, Jen led Jerry and Troy into the kitchen, where she poured each of them a cup of coffee and had a seat at the table.

"First of all, I want to make sure that you had a chance to speak with your friend about the situation," he said as he took a drink of his coffee.

After thinking for a minute to figure out what he was talking about, Jen nodded. "I spoke to him a few days ago, just before Yule, and he's agreed to leave them alone."

Troy looked confused, but Jerry smiled. "That's good. In that case, I think that having the pair of them stay here, even if it is only for a few days, will do them a world of good. But there are a few things that you need to be aware of, also.

"First of all, any rules of the house need to be explained to them clearly and before they've been here for too long. I think that tonight would be best, once they've had a chance to settle in just a bit.

"If they break any of the rules, I don't want them to get in trouble over it. If you can, try to talk to them about it and remind them that they weren't supposed to do whatever it was. Chances are they'll both try fairly hard to follow the rules but accidents happen."

"That makes sense. Although, I don't think

I have very many rules here that they need to worry about following."

"I wasn't sure, so I just wanted to mention it before it became a problem. Beyond that, if they could be given a chore or two around the house so that they have something to do, that'd be great for them as well. It doesn't have to be anything difficult, just something for them to focus on and be responsible for."

She thought for a moment. "I'm sure I can come up with something."

Before leaving, Jerry let her know that if she had any trouble with anything, whether it was the guys or if she just needed to talk, she was welcome to call him anytime, day or night. He handed her over a business card that had a number scrawled across the back in blue ink. "That's my cell number," he explained. "If nothing else, I'd appreciate a daily call for the next while, just so I can find out how they're doing." He grinned. "Also, don't be surprised if I drop in to see for myself."

Once she agreed, they headed off to see where the guys had gotten off to. They found them upstairs on the landing, where they were peering over the rail to see what was going on below. "Come on down, guys," Jerry called up to them. "Time for Jon and me to leave."

The troupe thundered down the stairs, and Jen was surprised at how quickly Bailey could move down the steps. If it had been her trying to crawl down them, she would have lost her balance and started to tumble by the third or fourth step and she knew it.

Jon stopped to give her another hug. "Thanks," he said while he held her tight. "I'll let you know as soon as we're ready to come get them."

"Don't worry about it," she answered. "You just worry about what you need to get done. They'll be fine until then."

He would have stayed to hold her longer, but Jerry gently pulled him away and guided him toward the door. "Let's let them get settled in, okay? You have a big day tomorrow."

Jen watched from the door as the pair of them climbed into Jerry's car. Once he turned the corner and was out of sight, she closed the door and turned towards her waiting guests. "Okay," she said. "There are plenty of snacks in the kitchen. You guys are allowed to have whatever you want, just try not to make too much of a mess out of anything. We'll worry about dinner in a couple of hours, after Patrick gets home." She explained that Patrick was her brother and had also been there when everyone was pulled out. "So you don't have to worry about him, okay?"

She pointed out where the bathrooms were, where the room that they would be sharing was and where her and Troy's rooms were. Once she was finished with that, Troy walked out to the living room with a board game. "Anybody want to play?"

Zack stepped forward and took a seat in front of the coffee table, but Bailey looked less enthusiastic about the idea. Seeing that, Jen had a seat on the couch and invited him up to join her to watch the game.

He climbed up next to her, curled into a ball, and hesitantly put his head in her lap. The pair of them settled down like that, with Jen stroking his hair, to watch Zack and Troy battle it out.

By the time Patrick arrived, Jen had started

to get hungry and was debating what to do for dinner. The problem was solved, however, as he arrived with a stack of pizzas. "Hope you guys like pepperoni, ham and pineapple, or just plain everything," he said as he set them on the kitchen table. "Because that's what I've got." He looked over at Troy as he opened the first box. "There's soda and breadsticks out in the truck still, would you go grab those?"

Zack stared at Patrick, his eyes wide and jaw slightly slack. When Jen noticed that, she scooted out from under Bailey to kneel at Zack's side. "What is it?" she asked.

"It was you," Zack said, his voice barely over a whisper and his eyes firmly locked on Patrick. He blinked a few times in rapid succession and turned to look at Jen, still wide-eyed. "That's your brother?"

Jen ran her hands over his shoulder and upper back reassuringly. "Yeah. It's okay, he won't hurt you. Nobody here is going to hurt you."

Zack shook his head and turned back to look at Patrick, who was looking over in confusion. "No, I recognize him."

"You do?" She looked between them curiously.

"He brought me out."

Jen smiled and smoothed his hair. "I told you he was there."

"I know; I just hadn't expected..." His voice trailed off as he spoke.

"Well, somebody had to," Patrick said as he dropped a few slices of pizza onto a plate. "You were kinda beat up, so I didn't think you could walk. Do you like pepperoni?"

Still looking slightly shocked, Zack nodded. "Thank you."

"Don't even worry about it." Patrick walked out with a couple of plates, both of which had a couple slices of pizza on them. He set one in front of Zack and handed the other to Bailey. "I wasn't sure what kinds you guys would like," he explained, "so I got a few different kinds."

Not for the first time, Jen was glad she had such a laid-back brother. It didn't seem to matter what happened, nothing seemed to faze him. She knew that he hadn't expected Zack to be one of the people he had personally carried out of the demons' lair but it didn't matter.

He would have reacted exactly the same as he would have had she brought home anyone.

Over dinner and sodas, things relaxed once again. Zack continued to look over at Patrick with an expression of amazement but neither of them pressed the issue and by the time everyone was ready for bed, nothing more had needed to be said. Jen led the boys up to the room that they would be sharing and tucked them both into the bed. Normally she wouldn't have bothered but Bailey had seemed particularly needy and she hoped that the extra attention would help both of them get a good night's sleep.

"If you need anything, I'm at the end of the hall," she reminded them. She left their door open enough to let in the light from the hallway, remembering the discussion where they had admitted to not liking sleeping in darkness.

Once she was sure that they would be okay, she headed to her own room to crawl into bed. Soon after pulling the covers up and getting comfortable, however, her door opened. Bailey silently crawled across her floor and up onto the foot of her bed. There, he curled up into an almost impossibly small ball, took a corner of the blanket, and settled down to sleep.

"Come on," she said as she lifted up the edge of her blanket. "You're not sleeping there." He didn't need to be told twice, as he climbed in next to her and settled down again.

Only moments later, her door opened again. Without bothering to ask, she lifted the covers on the other side for Zack to climb in as well.

I need to get a bigger bed, she thought to herself as she snuggled down between them to sleep.

Chapter 21

The next morning, Jen woke to Sahara standing over her, holding a pair of steaming cups of coffee. As Jen blinked, wondering if she had made plans to go out with her that morning, she reached out to take her cup. She propped herself up on an elbow and discovered that she was alone in bed, briefly wondering where the boys were as she took a sip.

"Are you aware you have a naked barista?"

"I what? Oh." That explained where Zack was but she was surprised that Bailey had gone off on his own. As she drank her coffee and tried to clear out the cobwebs, Jen explained what was going on. "So they're staying here for a few days while the rest of the group finds another place."

"Oh." Sahara seemed disappointed to hear the story. "I'd hoped that maybe you were having some sort of steamy, sordid affair or something."

Jen laughed. "Did we have plans today?" She asked as she took another sip of her coffee and sat up to stretch.

"No, I was just bored so I decided to see what you were up to," Sahara answered. "I should've known you wouldn't be out of bed yet."

Jen shrugged as she climbed out from under the covers. "It's not even noon, what were you expecting?"

Sahara snickered as she headed for the door. "I'll be downstairs when you're done getting dressed."

By the time Jen was ready for the day, her cup was disappointingly empty. She headed for the hall, intent on getting at least one more cup before Sahara dragged her off for whatever she had planned. As she reached the base of the stairs, however, Bailey was there to greet her.

"Hang on," she said as she stepped around him. "I'm not awake yet. I need another cup of coffee first."

Bailey lowered his head and turned to follow her into the kitchen. There, Jen was met by another unexpected sight: Zack had a deep purple bath towel wrapped around his hips as he sat at the kitchen table with his bowl of cereal.

As Jen blinked at him in surprise, Sahara explained. "It's from your bathroom. I figured that he should at least be covered when you have company."

"Are you okay with this?" she asked Zack, who nodded.

"She didn't exactly give me a choice," he explained sheepishly. "She just walked up with it and tied it onto me." As Jen continued to look at him in confusion, he shrugged. "It's not exactly clothes."

"Okay, as long as you're all right with it," she answered as she refilled her cup.

While she drank her coffee and worked on coming back to life, she absently stroked Bailey's hair and watched as Sahara puttered around the kitchen. "I have to admit," Sahara explained, "I like this kitchen a lot better than the one at your last place."

Jen shrugged. "What it needs is a bigger freezer."

"That's because you're convinced you can survive on microwave meals and coffee," Sahara retorted. "What you need is to find yourself a guy who can cook."

"No argument there," Jen agreed. "The last thing we need is for someone to try and teach me how to cook again."

"No kidding. Didn't you almost burn down half the town last time?"

"Only about a quarter of it."

As they teased back and forth and snickered, Jen realized that there were strange noises coming from outside. She picked up her cup to go see what was happening and got to the window just in time to see her Jeep launch across the lawn, heading toward the house. "Get down!" she yelled as loudly as she could.

Hitting the ground herself, she scrambled toward the drawer where she kept her duty pistol. Swearing as she heard the vehicle impact the side of her house, she pulled the key out of her pocket and retrieved the weapon; all of the rest of her equipment was either in the back of her truck or back at the office. "Sahara," she yelled, "get the guys out of here. And call my team!"

Without waiting to see whether Sahara was complying, she moved toward the door, joined swiftly by Troy, who had a rifle in one hand, a pistol in the other, and his bag of other assorted goodies hanging by its strap over his shoulder. "What's going on?" he asked.

"Psychic," she answered. "Did you call it in?"

"They're on live," he said as he indicated the phone on his hip. "David's getting the team rolling now."

As another explosion sounded outside, Jen reached for the door. She opened it barely enough to squeeze through and moved sideways as quickly as she could so that Troy could get out as well. Both of them could hear the psychic's maniacal laughter once they were out.

Jen had never felt as exposed as she did right then, lying on the snow-covered ground, dressed in only a pair of jeans and a long-sleeved shirt, with only her pistol and one clip to use against the psychic. As the snow melted through her clothes, she could feel the chill seeping through her, freezing her to her core.

Nevertheless, she had to move, and she had to move now.

Unfortunately, her yard didn't offer very much by way of cover. Prone on the ground, Troy dropped his bag onto the ground next to him and pulled the rifle around to take a shot. As they had before, the rounds bounced off an invisible shield that was a few feet in front of the psychic. Swearing, the hybrid switched clips and tried a different type of round. "Something's gotta get through," he growled.

He fired a few rounds from the new clip but they proved to be as effective against the shield as the first ones had been. Growling and snarling, he dropped his rifle and reached into his bag. With one hand he pulled out what looked like a homemade grenade and with the other he pulled out his blade.

With a howl, he pulled the pin from the grenade and was up and running before it went off. Unlike a regular grenade, when this one went off, it created a blindingly bright flash of light and a loud bang that echoed through the neighborhood.

As Troy moved across the yard, wielding his

hefty weapon to strike, the psychic turned his attention from Jen and directed it at the hybrid. After unleashing another of his powerful energy-bolt attacks, he scanned the area, apparently looking for a means of stopping Troy's rush. When his eyes fell on Jen's Jeep, which lay in a crumpled heap with all of its glass blown out and scattered across the yard in colorful, refractive shards, his grin widened and he released another peal of high-pitched laughter.

As Jen watched in horror, her truck lifted off the ground again, dripping more shards of glass and broken bits across the ground, leaving a clearly defined trail as it flew through the air at Troy. "Watch out," she screamed as her friend disappeared beneath two tons of ruined truck. Laughter assaulted her ears once more, bouncing around in her head like steel bearings in a pinball machine.

Jen felt a chill tear through her body that had nothing to do with the pile of snow that she was still lying in and somewhere deep inside, she felt something crack. For the briefest of moments and an eternity simultaneously, time stopped.

Slowly she stood up and turned to face the psychic. There was no sound except the faint rushing of her pulse in her ears and her own breathing, and even the cold barely registered in her consciousness. Time wasn't as fully stopped as she had initially believed. Instead, the entire world seemed to be moving in slow motion as she moved; even the snow was taking its time reaching the ground. The only thing that still mattered was the sight of the twisted carcass of her truck, which still lay on top of her friend. Even the sound of Zack and Sahara calling her name didn't matter anymore. She pushed it all aside and took a step toward the laughing corpse that had caused it all.

He sent a blast of his energy at her but in this new slow-motion world, she could track its trajectory as it flew and raised a hand to intercept it. The dark energy flowed down her arm and into her body, where she clenched it tightly inside her. Barely even looking where she was going, she took another step towards the psychic, followed by another and then another. A small voice in the back of her mind reminded her that Dr. McAdam had taught her how to dissipate, to release the energy once she took it, but she had different plans in mind.

Blast after blast launched toward her but she took them all. There was no pain, no cold, and barely even a hint of rational thought in her action as she methodically walked towards her target, accepting every assault he sent at her. Step after step, her foot sank into the accumulating powder, turning it to slush in an instant. Steam rose around her, which should have obscured her vision but somehow didn't.

Faintly she recognized that the energy that the psychic was throwing at her was a lot more powerful than the latent energy that she had absorbed until now. She knew that she wouldn't be able to hold onto it for very long, but she didn't need a whole lot of time.

She didn't plan to let the psychic survive long enough for it to become a problem.

As she moved even closer, the psychic launched more energy attacks at her, all of which were ineffective against Jen's fury. She felt the energy begin to leak and a small part of her paused, faintly remembering what had happened the last time she had lost control but she pushed it down. It didn't matter.

He backed away, obviously confused. He threw more of his energy blasts at her, almost haphazardly, as he tried to hold her off. She dropped her arm, no longer needing to hold it up to draw in the energy. Why had she never noticed that he was a one-trick pony before? For all the time she had been chasing him and trying to minimize the damage he was causing, she had somehow missed the fact that he really only had two powers to use: kinetic motion, such as what he had used to toss her truck around like a child's toy and his blue-gold energy blast that felt like nothing more than a mild electrical shock.

As she got closer, she could feel the energy that he had stored inside, and she targeted that, drawing the power out of him and adding it to her already overwhelmed stores. She felt more of the energy leak out but clamped down around it even more tightly. She knew that if she let too much of it escape, the psychic would just reabsorb it and that wasn't what she wanted at all.

Long before she reached the quickly-backpedaling psychic, she felt her hold on the energy slip again and the small part of her brain that had somehow maintained its grasp on sanity reminded her that she had to release it soon or it would kill her too. She stopped her advance, growling as she fought to maintain control.

Seeing her stop, the psychic made one last bad decision. He stepped closer, believing her to be a soft target, defenseless and completely spent.

He had no idea how wrong he was.

As she felt the energy fighting to break free from her, she focused all of her attention on the psychic, willing the blast to hurt him more than her. Closing her eyes and sending up a word of prayer for help to anyone who was willing to listen to her, she let go.

The blast tore out of her, dragging a scream out with it. She fell to her knees as the energy incinerated everything in its path. The snow on the ground, the grass beneath it, even the ice on the sidewalk and the frost that covered almost everything evaporated in an instant. The psychic barely had enough time to start to scream before he was thrown backwards by the sheer force of her blast, a direct hit with every bit of his own energy that she had taken from him. He slammed into a tree in the yard across the street from Jen's house, cracking its two-foot-wide trunk with the force of the impact.

The blue and gold energy continued to spark and crackle, illuminating the front half of Jen's yard and the yard of the house across the street. The light slowly faded as her power waned and Jen collapsed to the ground, completely spent. "I hope it doesn't land on me," she thought as the enormous pine tree, its trunk almost completely severed by the flying psychic, groaned in protest and crashed to the ground.

Dimly, she noticed a tall figure walking through the haze that blurred her vision. It stopped at her truck and almost effortlessly lifted it off of Troy's unresponsive form. Dropping the truck onto the lawn next to the hybrid, it turned and walked toward Jen.

She struggled to push herself upright, but couldn't move. As the figure stooped over her,

she could feel her consciousness slipping further away.

"Stupid woman," he said as she felt warmth
seeping into her body. "You should stop playing
with dangerous toys you don't understand."

She blinked at the familiar voice but wasn't
able to figure out who it was. For a moment,
she thought it was one of her teammates but
even as the idea floated into her head, she dismissed it.

The person lifted her so that she was sitting
up, wrapped securely in his arms. She relaxed
against his warmth, no longer caring who it was.
She was alive, and that was all that mattered.
More heat flowed into her, and she could slowly
feel herself coming back to life.

"You have to keep at least a little energy
inside of yourself," the mysterious voice explained. "Otherwise, you won't have enough to
survive."

By the time the fog in Jen's brain cleared
enough for her to look around and recognize
where she was, the stranger had disappeared.
She was lying on her back in a patch of bone-
dry and slightly warm soil, only a few feet

away from Troy's limp body. Somewhere in the distance, she could hear the reassuring sound of sirens but much closer she heard someone screaming. Not sure, she had to check to make sure the screaming wasn't coming from her.

She rolled over to her hands and knees to crawl over to him, ignoring the charred flesh on her hands where the energy had burned its way out of her. "Troy?" she rasped. "Troy!"

Although she had expected him to be dead, she wasn't prepared for the sight of him sprawled out in the only snow-covered patch left in her front yard. His legs and arms were twisted in unnatural angles and she didn't want to know how many times each of them had been broken. Beyond that, he looked just plain *flattened*.

To her amazement, as she moved closer to him, she could hear the raspy wheeze of his breathing. "Hang on," she said. "We'll get you to the doctor soon." Although she knew he couldn't hear her, she hoped that, at least on some level, he would be reassured by her words.

The sirens drew nearer as Marc, J.J. and the rest of her team ran into the middle of the chaos. Marc headed directly toward Troy, Mike and Ty went to be sure that the psychic was actually dead but J.J. made a beeline for Jen.

As Marc waved in the ambulance crews so that they could get Troy, J.J. tried to pick up Jen and take her over to another ambulance. "I'm okay," she said in a weak voice. "But Troy needs a doctor."

"He'll be treated too," he reassured her, "but you look like you've been blasted by the business end of a flamethrower."

Only then did Jen look down and recognize that the clothes she had only just put on were hanging off her in tatters. "I'll be okay," she insisted. "Sahara and the guys are still in the house. I need to let them know I'm okay."

"You're *not* okay," he insisted as he tried to pick her up again, but Jen wouldn't let him.

"Just make sure Troy's going to be okay, will you?"

"We'll be fine," Sahara called out the door. "Go to the hospital!"

Jen looked over at the sound of her friend's voice and realized that both of the boys had their heads peeked around her in the doorway.

Concern filled all three of their eyes, and Jen caved. "Fine," she said.

She let J.J. help her, insisting that she didn't need an ambulance. "If you want to just give me a ride, that'd be fine," she tried to explain, but J.J. didn't even bother to answer her.

He loaded her into one of the waiting emergency vehicles and Jen tried to relax as the medics began to swarm. As her mind cleared further, she realized that her feet were cold and her palms itched. No wonder, she realized as she looked down at herself. She wasn't wearing any shoes and there was strange black stuff flaking off of her hands and forearms. She tried to pull her hands together so that she could rub more of the irritating substance off, but for some reason the medics pulled her hands apart again.

She fidgeted all the way to the hospital, trying to rub her hands against the edge of the gurney and occasionally shaking her hair out of her eyes. There wasn't more that she could do until they arrived and she was lifted out of the ambulance and wheeled into the emergency department.

David and Charlie were already at the hospital, apparently waiting for her. She smiled ruefully at her boss as she was pushed past him and into a vacant room. "I wasn't playing Lone Ranger, I promise," she insisted. "He attacked me."

"I know," David reassured her. "Don't worry about that for now. Just relax and let the doctors do their thing."

"Troy's hurt bad," she said as she twisted to face him more fully.

"We know," David said as he pushed her back to a horizontal position. "Greg's all ready for him, so don't worry."

"That's good," she replied as she relaxed. If there was anyone she trusted to put Troy back together, it was Dr. McAdam. As another overwhelming itch overtook her, she vigorously rubbed her palms together, wondering again what the black stuff was. As it flaked away to reveal bright pink skin underneath, she figured it out. "I got burned?" she asked to nobody in particular.

David laughed. "You look like you got flash-fried," he said. "Like those greasy tacos you love so much."

She hadn't noticed that Charlie had left but he walked into the room mid-banter. "Sorry to interrupt," he said as he poked his head in the door, "but I heard this stuff was like an instant restorative to you, so I figured I'd better get you some quickly." He stepped into the room, carrying a tall steaming cup.

Jen accepted the cup curiously, sighing as she recognized the scent of freshly-brewed coffee. "Are you sure I'm allowed to have this?" she asked as soon as she had taken the first gulp.

Charlie grinned and nodded. "I talked to Greg and he said that as long as you didn't look dead when you showed up that we shouldn't worry too much. He wants to have a look at you before releasing you but at least you don't have to worry about having a whole new batch of doctors poking and prodding at you, since he's busy."

Jen sobered at that. "Do we know how Troy's doing yet? Is he going to be okay?" She couldn't quite bring herself to ask what she really wanted to know, to ask if he was still alive.

He shook his head. "Greg's with him right now, so I'm sure he's going to be fine. He's just too busy to talk right now."

Jen took another drink of her coffee. It wasn't a good answer but it was better than not knowing. Or worse, she realized. It would be a lot worse if there was nothing that even Dr. McAdam could do to save him.

The men kept her company, joined fairly quickly by the rest of her team, for the next two hours until Dr. McAdam came in to check on her. "I hear we had a bit of excitement to-day," he said as he stepped between the men.

Jen leaned forward anxiously. "How's Troy?" she asked. "Is he going to be okay?"

He smiled reassuringly at her. "He's stable for now but he's going to be hurting pretty bad in a couple of days or so. That's one tough friend you've got there." He nudged a couple more guys out of the way so that he could begin his examination. "What about you? How are you feeling?"

"Better," she answered. "I was pretty groggy for a while but I'm doing a lot better now."

She smiled up at him. "And there's only one of everybody again."

"That's a good sign," he said as he moved his energy into her. "I take it you forgot to dissipate like I taught you."

"Yeah," she admitted as she dropped her head. "I was kinda preoccupied so I wasn't even thinking about it."

"I can tell," he explained. "You've got a little residual damage from the blast, but it looks like it's healing nicely."

Chapter 22

J.J. offered to give her a lift once she was released to go home. They rode in silence for most of the trip, with him keeping a close eye on the road in front of them and her clutching her cup of coffee, which Charlie had graciously offered to refill for her before leaving. She glanced over at him a few times, trying to decide whether or not he was angry but decided not to press the issue.

When he pulled up in front of her house and parked, he left the engine running and turned to face her. "I want to know what's going on," he explained.

"With what?" she asked. There were a lot of things going on, and she wasn't sure which one he was referring to.

"When we got here, you looked like you had been set on fire. The last time we dealt with that psychic, you said you were taking his energy and now it looks like he lost one hell of an energy battle. Even more, the doctors didn't even bother to run any tests on you when you got to the hospital, almost like they knew that you were going to be fine without testing or treatment or anything else.

"Don't get me wrong," he continued, "I'm glad that you're okay and all but I really don't understand how you're able to do all these things all of a sudden."

"I don't completely understand it either," Jen admitted as she looked down into the inky depths of her coffee. "I know I'm not a mage or a psychic or anything like that but while I was over in Derathim, I could heal." She looked up at him as she explained further. "I don't know how, I just did.

"Then the dreamwalker, Steve, came to me and explained how to draw energy, so that's how I learned that one." She looked around at the ruined mess of her street. "That's what happened here, I took too much of the psychic's energy and I wasn't able to hold it all."

J.J. nodded slowly. "It's the same thing that happened when we came to get you, isn't it? There was a weird explosion when we were trying to break through, nobody knew what had caused it."

"Yeah," she admitted. "Dr. McAdam tried to teach me how to get rid of the energy once I take it, but I forgot today."

She looked up at him as she finished, still not sure how upset he was. "Are you mad at me?"

He looked over at her in surprise. "Mad at you? Why would I be?"

"I don't know," she shrugged. "You just look mad."

"No, I'm not mad." He reached out to take her shoulder and give it a careful squeeze. "I'm just worried, that's all."

She nodded, relieved. "Do you want to come in for a few?"

He shook his head. "I'd like to, but I've got a ton of stuff that I have to get done before I can knock off for the day. So you go ahead and get some rest, okay?"

She stepped out of the truck. She was inside the house and pulling the door closed behind her before she heard him pull away from the curb.

Sahara and the boys were in the living room, waiting anxiously on the couch for her to return. As soon as she stepped into view, Bailey was at her side. Even Zack got up to come over to check on her. She reached down to stroke Bailey's hair and gave Zack a hug. "I'm okay," she reassured all of them. "It looks a lot worse than it is."

"I sure hope so," Sahara said as she paused the movie that they had been watching. "Because you look like hell."

When she asked about Troy, however, her demeanor changed. Jen explained that he was stable but that he would likely be in the hospital for a while. "Go get Joel," she suggested. "I'm sure he's going to want to go check in on him too."

Sahara stepped back into her shoes. "Do you need anything before I go?"

When Jen declined, she headed for the door.

"If you do need anything," she called over her shoulder as she opened the door, "call me."

Once they were alone, Zack and Bailey guided Jen over to the couch so that she could sit down. Bailey scurried upstairs to find fresh clothes for her to change into while Zack fetched her a cup of coffee in her favorite cup. "Really, guys," she protested as they fussed over her, "I'm okay."

"You had better be," Thaxter said as he walked into the room. His face was set in hard lines and the casual smile that had frequently creased his face was absent. "That was careless."

Bailey whimpered and crouched low to the floor behind Jen, but Zack froze in place, shaking like a flag in a tornado. Seeing their reactions, Jen decided that Thaxter could wait, she needed to calm the boys down first. She reached down to Bailey because he was the closest and pulled him tight against her. "Shh, calm down," she murmured to him as she rested her cheek against his hair. "I promised you that nothing here was going to hurt you, didn't I?"

He looked up at her, his brown eyes enormous and quickly filling with tears. His glance darted to Thaxter for only a moment before returning to her again.

Still holding him close and smoothing his hair, she looked over at Zack, holding out a hand to him as well. "Come on," she encouraged him. "It's okay."

He looked as though he was trying to reach out and take her offered hand but couldn't seem to make himself move far enough. When she realized that he simply wasn't going to, Jen hoped she would have an easier time getting Bailey to move closer to him, hoping that they would feel safer when they were together.

Still clinging to her, Bailey inched closer to Zack, at her urging. Once they were both a decent distance away from the demon, Jen stepped in front of them and looked up to face the incubus. "You promised you wouldn't do this," she glared at him.

As he moved as though to take a step closer, Jen held up a hand. "Stay there, you've already scared them enough. Why are you here?"

"Because you almost got yourself killed again," he answered, but to her relief he didn't try to move any closer than he already was. "You need to be more careful."

She looked at him incredulously. "Seriously? You're here to bitch because I got hurt?"

"As I have told you before, you need to stop being so careless. One of these times, you're going to get seriously hurt."

"Look, I'm fine, okay? If that's all you're here for, then you can leave so I can get them calmed down the rest of the way."

"No, that's not all I'm here for. Once they discover that the psychic has failed, they will send out someone else."

"What?" her anger changed to confusion at his statement. "Once who discovers?"

"The Inquisitors," he said. He looked as though he would have said more, but he was interrupted by a knock at the front door.

Jen looked between the demon and her guys, not sure what to do. As she debated, the knock sounded again and she heard the door open. "Anybody home?" Jerry called out. "Is everybody okay in here?"

Jen swore. As if things weren't bad enough already, the last thing she needed was to have more people showing up. At least Jerry would hopefully help her calm the boys down so that she could get Thaxter out of the house. "We're in here," she called back to him. "Don't you move," she said warningly to Thaxter as the therapist stepped into the room.

Jerry took one look at the situation before hurrying over to where Jen stood between Thaxter and an obviously frightened Zack and Bailey. He tried to usher them out of the room, careful to not let them get close to the demon but the boys wouldn't move. Instead, all he could do was to sit with them against the wall and try to calm them as best he could.

Once she was sure that the boys would be okay in Jerry's care, Jen turned back to the demon. "I thought the Inquisitors only dealt with demons, so why do you think they're after me?"

"They are the ones that sent that one," he pointed outside, where Jen could still see the mess from the fight scattered across the block. "Once they realize he was ineffective, they will undoubtedly send someone else, someone more dangerous, to get the job done."

Jen blinked up at him in surprise. "But why would they be after me?" The only response she got from Thaxter was a shrug, so she sighed and sank into Troy's recliner to think. Even though the psychic hadn't spoken to her today, he had said some things the last time she had encountered him. She tried to remember everything that the psychic had said, finally looking back up at Thaxter. "Who's Maddock?"

Now it was Thaxter's turn to look surprised. "Where did you hear that name?" he asked.

"Is he one of them?" she asked. "Is this Maddock guy one of the Inquisitors?"

Grudgingly, Thaxter admitted he was. "If you know of him, that may explain why they are after you. How do you know him?"

"I don't," she explained as she stood and took a step closer to him. "The psychic mentioned him, said he was his master." She evaluated the demon thoughtfully. "Do all of you insist on being someone's master?"

He dismissed her last question. "Maddock was in the human world until only recently. I don't know what he was working on, but it had apparently been something important, as there was a lot of anger when he returned." He began to pace as he continued. "I don't know what caused him to return to our world so abruptly but he's been in a foul mood since his return."

Jen remained silent, waiting for him to continue.

"Furthermore, Maddock was the most vocal of the Inquisitors about the need to remove you." He looked over at Jen and smiled ruefully. "For whatever reason, he really doesn't like you. He was also one of the least pleased with my decision to keep you instead of just killing you as they had initially instructed me to."

"Whatever you did to him," Thaxter said as he stepped closer and took her by the upper arms to pull her to back her feet, "he really seems to hate you."

Jen wasn't sure how to respond to that but as it turned out, she didn't have to. Another knock sounded at the door and Jen scowled. As she shook herself free from the demon's grasp and headed for the door, she grumbled, wondering who had declared this to be Lets Be Social day. Her lack of amusement only increased as she opened the door and recognized who was standing on her porch this time.

"Miss Rice," Agent Thompson said as he smiled broadly at her, Agent Brooks directly next to him. "We'd like to talk to you, if you don't mind."

Not even bothering to answer, Jen pushed the door closed.

As the agents continued to bang on her door and yell to her through it, she headed back into the living room, where she saw that Jerry and Thaxter seemed to be in the middle of some sort of staring match. She blinked at the sight for a moment before stepping in between them.

"I think I've had about enough for today," she said as she looked from Thaxter to Jerry and back to Thaxter again. "You can leave by whatever means you want to; just get out for a while. I'll talk to you later, once everything's calmed down a bit." Then she turned to Jerry, who didn't wait to be thrown out.

"I'll come back later," he offered. "You guys need some time to process all of this." He looked back down at the guys, who were still huddled against the wall. "And I think you need to tell them what's going on."

Jen followed his gaze and nodded. "I'll call you later," she offered.

"You do that," he said over his shoulder. "I'll be waiting for your call."

Once both demon and therapist were gone, Jen turned to face the boys. "Come on," she encouraged them. She led them over to the couch, where all three of them collapsed in a heap. "I think we all need a break."

Chapter 23

Once Thaxter was gone, it only took about fifteen minutes for Zack and Bailey to calm down. Jen spent that time on the couch, holding both of them and reassuring them that they were safe, that nobody was going to take them back to the demon's realm.

"I don't understand," Zack said finally. "Why was he here?"

"He wasn't supposed to be," Jen admitted. "I talked to him before you guys came, to let him know not to come by while you're here." She explained that she and the demon had come to an arrangement, one that she had thought would suit everyone. "But you guys have nothing to worry about," she reassured them. "He's already agreed to leave you two, along with everyone else that was in that place with us, alone."

"But what about you?" Zack asked. "Why won't he leave you alone too?"

"I really don't know," she sighed. "But it's okay, you don't have to worry about me. He's not going to hurt me and, at least for the moment, he's playing by the rules."

Another loud knock sounded at the door and Jen swore quietly. She should have known that the agents wouldn't have given up so easily. After reassuring the boys that she was all right, she untangled herself from Bailey's arms and headed for the door.

"Ms. Rice, we still have questions."

She leaned against the jamb and crossed her arms, a clear signal that she wasn't interested in cooperating. "I thought we already covered this. I'm not interested in any more of your questions."

"We told you that we'd be back," Agent Thompson said with the most placating smile Jen had ever seen. "And so, here we are."

"Yes, I can see that. What I don't see is the warrant you were supposed to bring with you."

She knew that she was goading them, just as she had known it each time the obnoxious agents appeared at her door, but she didn't care. She'd had just about enough of their nonsense, along with everyone else's nonsense, for one day.

"Want to tell us what happened here?" he asked, gesturing to the mess in her yard. "Looks like a hell of a fight."

"Sure was," she agreed. "What I don't understand is why you guys always show up once the fighting is over? Where were you when the psychic responsible for all this," she gestured vaguely in the direction of her Jeep, which still lay on its side where Thaxter had dropped it, "was still here trying to kill me?"

"We came as soon as we found out what was going on," Agent Brooks interrupted. "Had we realized this was happening, we would have been here sooner."

"Fat lot of good it did to have you guys stalking me all the time," Jen grumbled. "Maybe if you guys were doing something useful instead of just harassing me all the time, Troy wouldn't be in urgent care at the hospital right now." She didn't bother hiding the disdain from her voice as she spoke. Although she knew that the agents weren't responsible for Troy's injuries, she didn't have anyone else available to blame at that moment and they made handy targets.

"We just need to know whether it was the demons that did this," Agent Thompson said. "If it was, then we can start working it from that direction but either way, we need to know."

"Demons?" she asked, incredulous. "You think this was demons? This was a human, a psychic. The same psychic that had been trying to kill me for the last number of months. If you want to know anything more about that, read the damned reports." Without another word, she stepped backwards into the relative safety of her house and closed the door.

It was only a matter of time, she knew, before the agents would uncover a reason to haul her away for their tests and who knew what else they would do. Until then, she was going to keep on living her life as best she could, doing her damndest to keep the people around her safe in the meantime.

Jen will return in

Path of Destruction

Available December, 2025

Keep reading for an exclusive sneak peek!

She had only barely settled into sleep when the dream hit her. She was in a large, wild-flower-strewn field that had a light dusting of snow across it. A light breeze blew, but it wasn't even cold enough to raise goose bumps on her arms. As Jen looked around, trying to figure out where she was and why she was there, a familiar form appeared at the edge of the field.

He was quite a bit shorter than her, with dark eyes and hair and a well-trimmed beard. He pushed a pair of thick, black-framed glasses higher onto the bridge of his nose as he jogged toward her. "There you are," he called once he was close enough.

A grin broke across Jen's face as she rec-ognized her friend. "Hey, Steve!" Steve Jen-kins was a psychic. More specifically, he was a dreamwalker and he had helped Jen to sur-vive and then escape from her imprisonment with the demons. Her excitement at seeing her friend again faded as she saw the expression of deep concern on his face. "What's wrong?" she asked.

"You must wake," he explained as he stopped

in front of her. "You must wake up and contact your friends. William is in grave danger."

"What happened?" She recognized the name; William was a vampire that Jen had met a short time ago. Although she wasn't particularly close to him, she still considered him to be a friend. "Is he okay?"

Steve shook his head. "No, he's not. You have to go, now. There is still a chance that you may save him, but only if you go to him immediately."

Jen didn't question him. Steve knew William far better than Jen did; in fact he had even sent the vampire to Jen when he had needed help and had no one left to turn to. Also, the dreamwalker hadn't ever led her wrong before, so she had no reason to doubt him now. Beyond that, if something had happened to William, she wanted to help.

She tried to ask Steve a couple more questions, but he waved them away. "There's no time," he stressed. "You must go. You will understand soon."

He shoved her hard enough to knock her over, but she woke before hitting the ground.

She sat bolt upright and blinked around for a moment before reaching for her phone. "Hey, Marc," she said as soon as her unit leader answered the phone, "we need to get the team rolling."

"What's going on?" he asked. He sounded as though she woke him up too, but that couldn't be helped. "Do you know what time it is?"

"Yep," she answered as she stepped into the jeans she had worn the previous day. They were still relatively clean, so they would just have to do. "William's in trouble."

Marc immediately sounded more alert. "What happened?"

She explained about the dream she had just woken from and, to his credit, Marc didn't question the validity of the message she had received. Not only had the rest of the team met Steve before, but his assistance had proved invaluable in facilitating the rescue of her and the rest of the demons' prisoners. "I'll get them going. Do you have an address?"

She ratted off the numbers, reading them directly out of the small address book she kept on her dresser. "I'll meet you guys there."

"Be careful," Marc cautioned her. "I'm not sure what class William is but you're only trained for class one Vamps, so you wait for the rest of us before you make contact."

"I know," she responded. Jen had gotten in trouble a few too many times about running into dangerous situations without waiting for the team to show up and she had no intention of taking on a vampire that was as potentially dangerous as William without backup. "I'll wait out front for you guys to show up."

Her little rental, a plain white hybrid sedan, waited in the driveway where the agency's representative had left it the previous afternoon. She hadn't been thrilled with it when they dropped it off, but she reminded herself that it was only for a limited time. Once her insurance paid out, she would get a real vehicle instead of this toy. When she had first laid eyes on it, she had half expected to see some sort of wind-up crank in the back to make it go forward like an old-fashioned vintage car toy she had played with as a child. For now, however, this was the best thing she had, so she climbed inside and fired it up.

At least she didn't have to wait for one of her teammates to come pick her up.

Unlike her truck, which had always announced its awakening with a loud snort and a throaty growl, this car barely made any sound at all. Jen had to look down at the panel of gauges to be sure it was even running. With a scowl, she shifted into reverse and backed out of her driveway.

As she cruised toward William's house, she discovered that the little car had a bit more zip than she had initially believed. When she stepped on the accelerator, the tires didn't howl like the ones in her Jeep had, but the car got up and *moved*. She pressed it even harder before taking the next corner and was rewarded with a high-pitched squeal and a lot more traction than she had expected. While the car leaned a bit in the corner, it didn't feel like it was about to fall over as her Jeep did whenever she took a corner a little too fast and all four tires stuck steadfastly to the ground. Grinning in spite of herself, she decided that maybe the people who spent all their money on import racers weren't quite as crazy as she had thought they were.

When she arrived at William's house, she had to slow down because J.J. and Marc were already there. She parked behind Marc's truck and jogged over to meet up with the men. J.J. Monroe was about halfway into uniform. The tall blonde had his black uniform pants on but rather than the matching shirt, he wore a red sweatshirt that had a black dragon chasing down one sleeve, advertising wear of the gym he belonged to. He grinned as Jen pulled up to park, his amusement at her new ride apparent. "What the hell are you driving?" he asked as soon as she stepped out onto the sidewalk.

"Shut up," she grinned as she jogged toward Marc. "Where are the others?"

"On their way," he said without looking at her. His attention was focused on the small, single-story house in front of them. "It looks pretty quiet," he said. "Are you sure that there's something going on?"

She nodded and followed his gaze. Although she hadn't ever been to William's house, the innocuous-looking place suited him. It was a pale butter yellow, with cream-colored accents and a handful of dark-stained wooden pieces.

Heavy draperies covered the windows, no surprise considering the nature of its occupant. A soft glow emanated from the light on the front porch, and there weren't any stray weeds growing out of the cracks on his walkway. The whole place was neat and tidy, exactly what she would expect.

"What've we got?" Mike asked as they jogged over to meet the rest of the team. He looked between Jen and Marc, as though he wasn't sure which of them he should be asking.

"Not sure yet," Marc answered. "I told you all everything we know right now." He looked away from the house to meet Mike's eyes. "But now that everyone's here, we can go find out."

As the unit leader, Marc led the pack up to the house, where he knocked on the door and opened it a crack. "Looks like it's not locked. Hello?" he called as he pushed the door wider. "New World Response; anybody home?" There was no answer, so he carefully stepped inside. "William? Can you hear me?"

Jen stepped inside directly behind him, calling for William as well. Unlike the exterior of the residence, the living room was a mess, with the coffee table overturned and magazines and other assorted papers scattered everywhere. Books were tossed all over the room. While a handful of them seemed to be recent editions, some appeared to be quite old indeed. As the team entered the house, they were careful not to step on anything, just in case it turned out to be evidence of something far more important than just a well-being check, which was what they were officially there for right then.

"What happened in here?" Ty asked as he looked around. "This place's been ransacked or something."

Jen nodded, wondering the same thing herself. William, who had always seemed to be so meticulous, didn't seem to be the type of person that would keep his home this messy. It stood at even more odds when compared against the exterior of the house. "William?" she called out to him again but there was still no response.

"Hang on a second," Mike called out to the group. "Does anyone else hear that?"

All of them stopped to listen, but slowly

each of them shook their heads. "No," Marc answered for the group. "What do you hear?"

"Footsteps," Mike answered as he stared at the ceiling. "There's someone on the roof."

Although Jen couldn't hear anything, she was willing to believe that he did. Mike had amazingly keen senses for a full-blooded human and there had been plenty of times where he had been able to detect things that the rest of the group hadn't. Without hesitation, she followed him toward the door.

Once outside again, the group stepped a short distance from the house so that they could see onto the roof. At first, Jen still couldn't see anything but an empty rooftop but soon a figure stepped over the threshold between the far side of the roof and the side that they could see. He was dressed in all black, but his clothes looked far too disheveled. His gait wasn't natural either, even considering the unsteady terrain of the roof, because he seemed to be stumbling and reversing his direction far too frequently.

As the group watched, wondering what to do, the wind shifted directions and blew towards them, so that they could hear him mumbling and muttering to himself. Although the words themselves weren't audible, the sound was still ominous. To Jen, he seemed to be fighting himself, as though he wasn't in control. A chill went down her spine as she realized the implications of that. "Hey guys," she said calmly without taking her eyes from the vampire, "I think he's about to rage."

After life growing up in the beautifully rainy Pacific Northwest, Shanon L. Mayer tends to keep indoors, writing story after story, building vivid worlds on paper while her thoughts hold everything but images. She tends to look at everything in her world for inspiration – especially her collections of skulls, dragon statues, swords and knives, and pretty much anything that fits her eclectic, geeky-gothic lifestyle.

When her busy life feels like too much, she can be found relaxing with a hot mug of tea and a documentary on anything from theoretical physics to deep ocean wildlife to the most famous heists the world has ever seen.